Glian, The Son of Nature

Glian, The Son of Nature

Shubham Basu

Srishti
PUBLISHERS & DISTRIBUTORS

Srishti Publishers & Distributors
Registered Office: N-16, C.R. Park
New Delhi – 110 019
Corporate Office: 212A, Peacock Lane
Shahpur Jat, New Delhi – 110 049
editorial@srishtipublishers.com

First published by Srishti Publishers & Distributors in 2007
Copyright © Suvam Basu, 2007

ISBN 9788188575602

Typeset in AGaramond 11pt. by Suresh Kumar Sharma at Srishti

Contents

Acknowledgements

I would like to thank my parents, my aunt at Nashville, my bigger family, my brother for always encouraging me to step into the bigger world.

I am thankful to all my friends, especially Valli and Animesh for always being the first ones to read my stories, and actually approve them.

I think I am the reflection of the all the impressions I have had in my life, all the things I have witnessed in my life, voluntarily or involuntarily. I mark the next few pages, as an ode to the mighty creation, which is a witness to all life, thoughts and impressions. I dedicate this to that supreme soul of all impressions and life, Mother Nature. I thank her for making me capable of being guided by the instinct bestowed by her.

1

Getting the backpacks ready

I, Dev, have just returned to India from New York City. I have given up my job and career there, for my sweet home India. My spirit had been haunting me for a long time and finally it got me by my throat when one fine morning I made the decision. As the airplane landed in New Delhi I breathed in fresh aspirations to travel and explore. I was burdened with ideas and eager to take them off my shoulders, one after another. I joined my first job in India and waited for the first opportunity to take off. I was athletic, strong and completely into sports. I loved travelling and had travelled a lot in USA and India. I prefered the greener pastures more than concrete. However I hold the spirit of ancient ruins in high esteem. I would occasionally get lost in the dream that keeps looming at such places.

Luckily, my first opportunity came a month later. I had planned a small vacation with Ravi, my old schoolmate. Ravi was married and had a kid. I did not have to work hard at convincing him, to leave his baggage behind. I asked him to be ready for a binge at full throttle. It was March and we decided to go over to a small village Chundi, for our time out. We did not want any body else to know where we were heading and had decided to pick our destination at the last moment. The day before we started, we got busy grinding our heads on phone. In the end however, I won, owing to my longer relationship with travel. All said and done, we wanted to travel by the most local means. Ravi had a hard time digesting the fact that a time out vacation would be wasted in a village, but I had my arguments.

"I will show you a life of fun you never have had before. Four days."

"How the hell do a vacation and a village go hand in hand?" Ravi argued and that made sense.

"Have you ever been to a village?" I talked with the eye of a professional. With my new d-SLR I certainly was getting a keen eye.

"You don't want me to be a scapegoat to your wants right?" The surprising rebuttal came up.

"See I have lived in cities big and small, but somehow I find all the peace and oneness in such humble back countries. Come up, you will enjoy it. People think places like Dubai, Singapore, NYC are stress relievers, but they are stressful by their own means. What you need is some time to relax and be with yourself. Peace of mind comes in silence and serenity. You find it when you are closer to nature." Somehow I had convinced Ravi, but he chose to be skeptical.

Since it was my call, we finally concurred. We started packing. I had my EMS back pack which could have been packed better to stuff two more shirts in, but I was hardly good at it. My camping gear was stuffed in another bag and ready to be hitched with my back pack.

"Why do we need the camping gear?" Ravi shot the question, now suspicious of my intentions.

"Have you ever camped before?"

"No."

"Well, we might not actually camp, but this is in case of emergency." I thought this was the best answer, to avert any direct questions.

Ravi got his own back pack ready.

In India we always find plenty to eat around, so we did not actually bother to pack tinned food. However I always kept a provision for emergencies. I picked a pack of crackers and jam. Ravi kept throwing suspicious glanses at the thoughts of surviving on crackers. I could feel that it was best to leave as quickly as possible before he changed his mind. I wondered, whether I was actually forcing it on Ravi. Some people are not so comfortable with that kind of a survival. Still I wanted to tease Ravi.

"Hey Ravi, I have an idea."

"What idea now?" Ravi had already given up.

"Let's ride our bicycles to that place."

That was enough to release all the steam. The expression on Ravi's face changed from being serious to a big thunderous laugh. It took him five seconds for that transformation.

"Ha, Ha…you must be kidding."

I left it at that. I checked out the panniers in sight. Biking would have been fun.

"Know what Dev, what would have been real fun?" Ravi had the glimmer in his eyes.

"What?" Dev certainly was curious, the idea better be good.

"If the two girls staying next door could give us company."

I pondered over the idea. It certainly was a good thought. Ravi had talked sense finally. I preferred travelling alone. The idea is to meet strangers along and make new friends. I wasn't a real proponent of the idea of carrying known people along as baggage. It reduces the exploration part. Still, the neighbours were a pair of pretty girls, both working at Delhi, young, aged about twenty seven. Once in a while I spent time watching some movie with them. I was choosy, so most often the girls would end up watching what I liked. Moreover since I was much involved in sports and adventure, people certainly looked up at me with respect and mere curiosity was the reason for people to spend some time my way. "What motivates Dev?" is what a lot of people often thought. Though it had only been a little over a month that I had been living there, a lot of people saw me running in the mornings or disappearing with my bike loaded with panniers on a sunny Saturday morning and appearing back only on Sunday nights. Nevertheless, asking the neighbours then would be interesting. Two guys, two girls, a whole hoard of experiences and emotions. I thought of the prospects, of new thoughts for my writes.

"Well, absolutely, a grand idea. But would they really want to go out?" I wondered.

"They are your friends, ask them." Ravi assured

"But, it's so sudden…"

"Isn't that your way, sudden surprising things, more fun, more the merrier, new experiences…"

I cut Ravi short.

"Mmm. Let me try." I sat straight on the chair, right next to my back pack.

"What are you thinking now?" Ravi impatiently asked.

"Scheming. Remember…Give him an offer he can't refuse."

"Ya ya. And what would that offer be?"

"That's what I am scheming."

"Schemes, to get the company of those girls. Marvellous prospects. And the heck, a married guy can't try, but if it comes, he can't refuse, can he?"

"Don't dream. If you get their company, that is all you would get. Better to keep it straight. As it is you have had a bad one recently."

"Oops, the steam eh!"

"No man, you are a day ahead of me. They should be ready to ride along first. I don't even know if they are back packers." I expressed my concern.

"I am ready to camp." Ravi announced.

"Ready to camp…where is the five star guy now?" I gave the surprised squeal.

"How many people can sleep in the camp?" Ravi smiled.

"Well, four, and comfortably."

"Yeah baby, I will sleep between those two."

"You better keep your hungry teeth in. Won't kick a mouse in bright day light but ready to stomp an elephant."

"What's the harm in dreaming? I enjoy pretty babes."

"Yeah, if you really want to enjoy you should be Neil Cassidy. Did you read any Jack Kerouac?"

"Jack Kerouac who?"

"Knock Knock who. Give it up."

"Ha ha. I have never been the reading guy, you know that."

"Yeah you have been frenzy all your life."

"Alright cut the crap. Are you going to ask them?"

"I don't even know if they are home."

"Here call them. Do you need the number too?" Ravi got up and picked the wireless phone up.

"Alright see, I am skeptical. I hate to take no for an answer." I sighed.

"How do you know they would refuse? I saw the one, what's her name, the one with shorter hair...C'mon who is she?"

"Rimi."

"Yes Rimi. You remember the other night when you were sitting on that stool, in your boxers." Ravi looked at me.

"I saw her staring at your thighs. Man she had that lust in her eyes." Ravi's eyes were sparkling.

"She can't refuse." He stood up and walked to me.

"And if one goes, the other one goes too. The other one, yes Jane, she is. Wow what a bunch, one Assamese the other a Christian. Oh my god, can god be more benevolent?" He pulled out his index finger and poked me straight at my heart while he emphasized.

"What so amazing about their religion?" I asked.

"Well, you know hidden desires. Never been to Guwahati, but I have a feeling that the girls there are hot. So must be their attitude. And beautiful Kerala, the soft pacifying lifestyle. Jane is not just Jane, she is the entire Kerela to me. Frankly speaking, having you as a friend, has enhanced my curiousity in lifestyles too."

"Why, a little while back you weren't even ready to go to Chundi."

"That was different. Two guys. What can they do? But with the girls, it can be sure shot fun."

"Atleast you have started thinking."

"Man you are wasting your time thinking. C'mon call them up."

"Should I really? We are supposed to leave tomorrow even before the day breaks, they won't be able to prepare themselves."

"Then we will leave later."

"The point is that they might need more time, they might have plans already."

"Unless you ask them..." Ravi was grinding his teeth.

I picked the phone up. As soon as I was going to dial, the phone rang. I clicked the talk button.

Ravi heard the distant female voice on the phone.

"Dev, This is Rimi."

"Rimi, Hey what's up."

"Hey, I don't know if I should be saying this but I don't know who I should talk to at this hour."

" Why what happened?"

"Its one in the night and Jane isn't back yet."

"What?"

"I tried calling her friends, but nobody knows. I am really worried for that girl."

"That's serious."

"And I am damn scared. I talked to Atul and he says that I should call the police."

"Well may be that would be the right thing to do. Are you all by yourself?"

"Yes."

"Wait, let me come over."

I hung the phone. Ravi stared at me.

"You heard everything right?"

"Ya, caught most of it."

"Let's go to her place."

As we rose to walk to the door, the bell rang. Rimi was standing outside. Her eyes were wet. She dragged herself in and I thought I needed to comfort her. I hugged her and patted her head.

"Wait we will do something."

She started wailing even harder. Ravi gave up his seat and we made Rimi sit down. She sat with her legs tightly close to each other, body snuggled, giving a feeling as if she were cold. I thought it was the fear she was going through, oblivious of any other thing around.

"Let me make some quick tea. Will help us think better." Ravi volunteered.

The tea came as she scanned the room. She saw the back packs against the wall, the shoulders straps towards them.

"Are you guys heading somewhere?" She gathered enough courage to ask.

"Were supposed to." I answered while Rimi stared at the floor.

"But not until we find Jane." I sat down on my knees with my hands on hers and looked into her eyes.

"Where can she be?" Ravi asked the general question to put their thoughts back to the vital issue. He hardly knew anybody in her circle.

"Yes, where can she be?" I wondered, trying to recall everything I knew since the last one month of knowing my neighbours.

"Can you think of anybody else we can call?" I asked Rimi.

She gave a blank look.

"Have you called all your friends?"

She nodded her head. I picked up her cup, which she hadn't touched, and placed the warm cup in her hands, feeling her hands again.

"Keep drinking." I knew how assuring touch could be at such moments.

"She did have a boyfriend right?" I asked her.

"Not after her last break up." Rimi looked more composed.

"And we can't just call people up at one in the night, especially an ex-boyfriend." I concluded.

I walked to the window and looked through the blinds, eager for the night to pass.

Ravi could actually do nothing more than being an audience. I, on the other hand, could do no more than make suggestions and make the girl feel comfortable.

"We might have to wait till the morning to do the next thing, but let's keep thinking." I suggested.

"But where did she go? I am just scared about something bad…" Rimi's fear spoke

"Anything can happen, but it's unlikely. She is smart and knows how to take care of herself." I put up some assuring defense.

"Yes, smart enough not to call her roommate and just let her know."

I went on to seat myself on the couch. Rimi followed and sat on my side. Ravi kept himself seated on the lazy boy. Rimi dowsed off on my shoulders. Ravi checked his watch. Five in the morning.

The ring on the phone woke everybody up.

I picked it up and in my drowsy voice, announced my presence.

"Hello."

"Dev is that you?"

"That's me."

"Hey this is Jane. Do you happen to know if Rimi is home?"

I looked at Rimi. She was sitting wide awake.

"She is here, at my place."

"The devil, I have been trying to reach her all night. What is she doing there?"

"She got scared when you did not return late and came to my place around one, worried like hell for you."

"But she should have at least kept the phone next to her. Listen I am in a hurry; I had to go to Jaipur suddenly. My friend is ill. I will call Rimi back later."

Jane hung up.

"Ha, there you go. What a nice situation." I walked to Rimi and kept my hand on her shoulders. "Are you feeling alright now?"

She put her hand on mine and shook her head.

"A lot." She thought again. "I should have kept the phone next to me."

I walked to the window and looked through the blinds, it was a bright morning. The day had already broken. We had missed the right time.

"Do you guys have to go out now?" Rimi asked.

"We were supposed to."

"Well in that case I should take off now." There was sadness in her voice.

"Do you want to come along? Anyways you don't have anything at hand and always wanted to go on a trip with me." I asked her sincerely, as I shrugged my shoulders, validating my sincerity.

"Where are you going?"

"Well even we don't know for sure now. But we will go where all three of us want to go."

"Well, I don't want to be a burden on you."

Ravi was up, staring through his half closed eyes.

"Not at all, it's our pleasure." Ravi said, all his sleep disappeared.

"Remember what I say, the more the merrier, and more experiences. See the entire night was so much of a lesson for me." I added.

"For your stories?" Rimi asked mischievously.

"Well yes, I derive inspiration from such incidents." I repeated the same words that I did so often.

We helped Rimi pack. As we locked our houses and started, Ravi looked at me. I could read the look in his eyes.

"No Jane for you. Hard luck buddy." I responded in Ravi's ears.

2

Where are we going?

We, the pack of three walked out of the door. We looked around, the fresh morning breeze was rejenuvating. A bunch of monkeys were skipping from one roof to the next.

"Look at that monkey, over there." I exclaimed.

Ravi and Rimi turned to look to their right.

"Do you guys see what it is feeding on? Gosh, it's eating grass. That fails me guys. Who has the explanation?" I looked at Ravi. Rimi might not have been the ideal candidate to answer the question.

"It must be a renegade." Ravi declared calmly. I wondered why it did not arouse his curiosity. I had never seen a monkey eat grass before.

"I think the monkey is sick." Rimi came up with the idea. "I have heard that even tigers can eat grass at times. In fact I was reading about carnivores eating grass some times once in a while." She looked at me expecting support. "Do you see how selectively it is digging the grass up? It knows which ones to pick."

"Instincts; that's all they have right? No doctors, no physicians." I was amazed.

Rimi smiled, while I watched Ravi's stupid face. It's tough arousing his interest. I could expect this. Jane was missing.

"Would you guys mind if I asked my cousin out with us?" Rimi thrust the sudden question. It seemed as if she was eager to table it for a while.

"Would it be a he or a she?" Ravi jerked his head back.

"She is Richa. I just told her about our trip. She wanted to know if she could join."

"When did you talk to her?" Ravi asked, unable to figure out the fall of events.

"I did, a few minutes back."

"Why sure, she is welcome." I voiced, even before Ravi could. I caught him with his mouth open. "Is she as active as you are? And how old is she?"

"She is a year younger to me. I don't think that she has ever made such a trip though." Rimi looked at me with a very eager face. "Would that be a problem?"

"It's never a problem. We can always accommodate. One has to start somewhere." Ravi's sermon followed.

"How many times have you?" My looks suggested, as I looked at Ravi.

"Can she come down here? Or should we pick her up?" I asked.

"I think she can come down here. She lives a few blocks down. Haven't you seen her? The bright yellow Santro."
"Ah, right. I know who you are talking about. Alright make the call, quick. She has to get ready as fast as she can. We are losing time."

Rimi called Ruchi up and did her usual womanly chit chat. It had a different flavour though. Usually, I have seen women do that at leisure. That sounded better. The flip side would be worse though.

"Wow that was fast." I commended her ability.

"Fast? Means the way I spoke over the phone?"

"Yeah, I could hardly follow you."

"Eavesdropping has never been a good idea; but now that you were, tell me what language was I speaking in?"

"I thought hindi."

"No."

"C'mon Ravi, you saw it. You heard what I heard. What do you have to say?"

Ravi had a big grin on his face.

"I thought it was a mix of Maithili and Tamil."

"Wow Ravi, you are really good." Rimi smiled at Ravi.

"Years of experience."

"At least you are good at something." Suddenly a thought struck me. "Oh my God. Don't tell me your ex-Tamil girl friend was partly a Bihari aborigine."

Ravi had that stupid smile back on his face. I shook my head in disbelief. How many girl friends had he had?

"Did you know Rimi that this guy has had eleven girlfriends in his life?" I started a new topic.

"Twelve, to be precise. And we need not discuss them." Ravi was clear enough in his ordeal.

"Wow! Twelve." Rimi's eyes certainly looked bigger.

"I am not discussing. Rimi is curious. We can atleast tell her the good part."

Ravi stared at me. He had become an object of fun after his marriage, just because he had no way left to carry on with his romantic venture.

"Each of his girlfriends hailed from a different locale in India.

A new language, costume, lifestyle, everytime." I smiled as I felt him envy me.

"Wow. It must have been very interesting." Rimi added.

"Forget it Rimi, you don't stand a chance. He already has a Delhite on his roster. He doesn't repeat."

"I am not a Delhite. I am from Guwahati."

"Still, hard luck. He already is ..."

Before I could speak another word, I felt a big stomp on my foot. I held my foot in my hands and kept skipping on the other, in pain. Though in my shoes, I kept blowing on it. I liked exaggerating.

"Are you alright?" Rimi asked.

"Now you are the villain." I winked at Ravi.

"Why, why is he a villain?" Rimi asked.

"Just for fun. No harm in assuming."

"By the way, why don't we go and sit over there, while your cousin gets here." I pointed out to a shelter under a tree. It had a good place for sitting, made out of cold white stone. "Ya, let's not go back in again, now that we are out."

The three of us walked to the tree.

"Do you guys know what kind of tree this is?" I asked. I was trying to improve myself in identifying species. My mountaineering courses were coming up. It always helped to know as many species of flora and fauna one knew, especially since I travelled a lot.

"Will you put a lid on that curious mind of yours? Don't bore us." Ravi summoned. "By the way it's a simple version of Cacacia Actacia."

"Cacacia Actacia. What a name. How do you know all that?"

"I don't"

"But you just said it."

"Stop asking questions and remember the name. I will ask you again tomorrow."

"You made it up, didn't you?"

"Why should I make it up?"

"I know you. You won't know all this. You will be punished for this."

I tickled him to glory. He tried stopping me. But it wasn't any help. He was leaner than me in school days. After marriage, he had put on weight, giving me more surface to ply on.

"Stop doing that."

"Swear you won't lie."

"See what you did to my shirt."

Ravi's shirt was out of the neat confinement of his trousers and belt.

"Now you will have to pay for this." He was ready to avenge himself.

He put his back pack down and ran after me like crazy. We ran around the Acacia Cactacia in the parking lot. Rimi sat there laughing. Ravi was soon tired after the long run. I knew he could never catch me. Running was what I was good at, not him. Though, he might be stronger that I was. I won't risk challenging him at that. We were far off from the tree. Rimi wasn't in audible range any longer. We were standing right over a concrete plank, laid over a narrow nullah. We could feel it swing like a see-saw, as we shifted our weights.

"Why don't you try the tickle part on Richa, when she comes." I suggested as I laughed.

"Why don't you kiss my ass?"

I kept laughing, and Ravi joined. Joginder aunty was taking her morning walk, with her pet dog. Both stopped to look at us.

"You guys can laugh like anything."

"Joginder aunty, good morning." I greeted her.

Joginder aunty was a short woman. Her short stature wasn't her signature though. Punjabi by birth, she could speak in Bengali and Gujrati, equally fluently. Reason, her husband was a Bengali, and she has lived in Gujrat for a long time. She made sure she told everybody about it. That's how I knew. She had been a teacher and then a principal at the Delhi Public School, in the neighborhood. More than fearing her, I respected her. I suspected that her experience with kids would expose any contraband instincts in me. I tried being as honest as possible, with her. Her presence reminded me of all the punishments I had taken at the principal's office, as a kid.

"Carry on boys. Laughter is the best medicine."

The doggy kept looking at us. It somehow took a lot of interest in Ravi. It was pulling hard at the leash, in its attempt to smell him.

"See even the doggy knows that something is wrong."

"Obviously, I am a stranger here."

"Joginder aunty how is your morning gathering on? Do you people still do the laughter thing?"

I used to see them do a very dynamic laughter, at a park, down the lane. In fact, I joined them once. I took me a while to catch up with them. It had taken them years of practice to get there.

"Yes son. Perfect. Your uncle has started jogging these days. I don't know what you told him, the last time you came over."

"Oh, all that. Good for him aunty. He will stay trouble free. You need not send him to the garage for any over haul soon. Give him my greetings aunty. And tell him that next week we will go jogging together."

"Yes son, I will. Why can't you take that stupid son of mine with you? All he does is sleep and watch television."

"He is hardly twelve, aunty."

"Whatever. You guys, carry on now. The doggy wants to poop."

We left Joginder anty and her pooping doggy. We walked back into the parking lot and headed straight for Rimi. She was looking out for us. I looked at my watch.

"We are past twenty minutes, already." I noticed.

Upon getting closer to the girl, we noticed her playing with a white flower.

"What flower is that?"

Rimi shrugged her head. She was wearing a pair of cream colored slacks and a light green tank top. The necklace made out of wooden beads looked great on her. The beads were larger at the center, and smaller as they went around her neck. The largest bead took the spot right between her breasts. I looked at her. I had never known that she could look so pretty.

"Rimi, why don't you look like a Guwahatian?" I just asked. I needed an excuse to keep looking at her.

"And how is a Guwahatian supposed to look"

"More like a Mongolian."

"How does a Mongolian look?" Rimi laughed.

"Do you know who Timur the lame was?"

"Why, the women look like him?"

"Like his wife."

"His wife must have been pretty."

"Pretty? No body has a count as to how many he had."

"What rubbish?"

"When he went on a drive to plunder and spread his empire, he always made sure that he left a sapling of his Mongolian blood, running in the grounds."

"Oh is it?"

"He was a big tyrant. He was brave though. I guess the brave have the rights to trophies."

"What about you? How many trophies would you want?"

"That question would be for Ravi." I looked at Ravi. He shook his head. "He already has taken a big one home. He had to put up a lot of fight."

"Oh is it? Ravi, I would really want to know."

"There is nothing to it. It's a fight unto naught. There is only darkness beyond the horizons." The attention span on Ravi made him uneasy.

"Why do you say that?"

"Huh!" Ravi sighed.

"Rimi, why don't you tell Ravi about your love life?"

"Please Dev, not now."

"It's a short and sweet story. Do you want me to help you?"

"No." Rimi blushed. Her cheeks were as red as cherry.

"Later."

"Alright then. We will have to do something while we wait. Let me start. I will tell you about my uncle, Barin Chaudhury. I read this from his diaries. It has left a remarkable impression on me. I just wonder whether life was more complicated then, or is it now?"

"Please, no stories." Ravi exclaimed. "Atleast don't relate it your way. Try something else."

3

My uncle Brain Chaudhury

Tiku threw the first stone into the lake, it bounced thrice before it actually sank in. He had been hearing about the magic of flat stones and had been practising throwing them. He was preparing to move to his next lesson. The village had a new teacher, young, perhaps too young to be a teacher. People said that he had left a very promising job at Calcutta and adopted this new life. Barin Choudhury, PhD in Physics from Calcutta University, 1962. This is only what he knew about his teacher, for he never asked anything beyond it. His tricks and lessons were too fascinating and time consuming for Tiku to take interest in any other area.

"Master babu! Look at this one, how many bounces?"

"Should make at least five, if you throw it right."

Tiku threw it at an elevation which was a tad over horizontal.

"One, two, three, four, five." Tiku counted.

"So you seem to be getting on well with it."

"But I saw you throw with nine bounces."

"That takes time Tiku, everything takes time. The first three bounces are easy to get, things start getting difficult after four.

Keep practicing." Barin examined another piece of stone, and kept it on the ground. He looked at a burrow in the mud. Still bent, he looked at Tiku, who was still throwing his stones. "Tiku,"

".×.five, six... yes Master babu."

"Come here."

"Six bounces." Tiku counted before he advanced towards his teacher.

"You will improve." He turned his head towards the burrow. "Look at this."

Tiku came closer, "That is a scorpion hole, is it not?"

"It is, but there is something else about it."

"Something else; what would that be?" asked Tiku, never doubting a single thing that the teacher said.

"It's waiting for its prey. Come here, look from this position."

Tiku looked at the burrow.

"Do you see something?"

"Yes, I think I can see it. What is it doing?"

"It is ready to pounce upon a prey. And if you dare to stamp on the hole, bare foot, you can as well take the sting."

Tiku looked at it again.

"Let's go now."

They kept silent for a while.

"Master babu, everybody asks why you came here."

"What do you say to everybody?"

"I tell them that Master babu loves the green trees in our village."

"Then let it be that way."

"Ma says that you had a big job?"

"How do you define big?"

"Means...."

"Means big as in a big balloon or a big airplane?"

"Big as in a big ship."

"What else is big?"

"Big? This world is big, the sky, the moon, the sun."

"Are you big?"

"Me, no I am still small, not even eight."

"Suppose that scorpion sees you, what would it think of you, big or small?"

"Big"

"Then how big is big?"

Tiku made a face, perhaps unable to truly comprehend the issue of being big.

They heard a distant sound of an engine roaring. They turned to look and saw a car coming towards them.

Barin kept looking at it while Tiku looked at the car, and then his master looking at it. The car stopped close to them and an elderly gentleman stepped out. He came close to Barin.

"What are you doing here father?"

"I came to the village and came to know that you were sitting around the lake." He looked at Tiku. "Is this the young kid, Tiku?"

"My name is Noren Haldar."

"Noren Haldar. That is a fine name." He looked back at Barin. "I came to take you back with me."

"Father, I already told you that I am not going back."

"Barin, your mother is ill. She wants to see you."

"What happened to her?"

"She survived a stroke two days back. She is stable now, but keeps insisting on seeing you. She finally pushed me to bring you back today."

"When you have come so far, won't you want to see where I live?"

"We have to leave before two in the noon. But we still have an hour."

"Tiku, go back home. I will go with my father."

"Ok. Are you teaching tomorrow?"

"If I don't, I will leave a message with your mother."

"Are you going back to Calcutta?"

"Go back home now, it's not the right time to ask questions."

Tiku left through the bushes. Barin and his father sat in the car and directed the driver on the mud tracks.

"This is not the right spot to get your car in; still I am ready to take the risk to save time."

"The roads in this village are much better than Sona village. There you never know where you would come across pot holes and swamps."

"Barin." The father looked at his son seriously. "The High Commissioner has been asking about you." He pulled out his box of betel leaves. "I did not know what to say." He took one out and thrust it into his mouth. "It's awkward when people ask so many questions. Its better to keep them shut. But the Commissioner is not people, he is the Commissioner. What am I supposed to tell him when he asks me as to why you are ruining your career, for a mere village woman?" He looked out of the window. "What is wrong with you…?"

"Father, you don't want to get started again, do you?" Barin cut him short.

"Get started, I am getting started. I talk sense to my son and he says that I am getting started."

"Stop right near that well." Barin instructed the driver.

They got out of the car. There was exasperation in the eyes of the father. Barin led him to a small house and pushed the door open.

"This is my home father."

"Do you have any light inside?"

"Malati gets me a lantern every day at around six in the evening. There are still a couple of hours before she brings one." He walked to window and opened it. "Here, now we have enough light."

"Do you cook yourself?"

"No either Malati gets it or sends it with Tiku."

"It seems that over the span of a month you have become a celebrity around this place."

"People respect me, that's all."

"Do you try to tutor them in physics and the laws of science?"

"They won't understand."

"Precisely, they won't understand. So why the hell are you trying to waste all your knowledge here?"

"Father, I have already said I don't want to talk about it."

"Why don't you? Must I not know the reasons for such a drastic decision in your life?"

"I would have answered father, but I can't. There is a lot at stake."

"My respect is at stake. The son of a Minister stays in a village, with the rustics."

Barin saw Tiku stand at the door.

"What is it Tiku?"

"Ma sent tea and sweets for your father."

"Come in and leave it here."

"Father, how was the journey?"

"I told my assistant to tell every body that I am sick."

"What is it Tiku?" Barin looked at Tiku. He was still around.

"Ma was asking whether she should prepare dinner for your father too."

"Yes, for both of us."

Barin was still looking at Tiku.

"She was also asking whether you would be teaching at the evening school today."

"Tell her that I would keep a little busy today." He was still looking at him. "And you may go now."

Tiku slipped out.

"Does that kid stay with you throughout the day?" Barin's father asked.

"Yes, and you won't believe if I tell you how intelligent he is. There are so many kids like him who waste away their intelligence, due to lack of opportunity, or just because they were born poor, in a poor part of the country, or may have been born rich but were abandoned."

"Is he abandoned?"

"Kind of."

"Where is his father?"

"He died in the 1971 war."

"It seems that the villagers take good care of you."

"Yes father, every evening I get my dinner here or whichever house I am at. They are all so loving."

"Why don't you start packing?"

"What packing?"

"I see, you have hardly anything here. But I believe your mother has already made all arrangements. Though the doctor asked her not to move, she could barely wait for me to leave."

"I have to come back here father."

"Yes you can come and visit these people whenever you want to, moreover the Commissioner said that he would be more than willing to give the job back to you."

"I am not talking about visiting father. This is my home now."

"Don't talk rubbish. This is not where you belong."

"Even Malati doesn't belong here father. Still, she is living here."

"What does Malati have to do with it?"

"Father let's not go over it, let's not argue. Let's accept that I want to stay here, in this village, and let me live my life the way I want to."

His father had started shaking his leg in restlessness and anger.

"I told your mother, that the donkey of a son that she has brought up, would never listen to me. He is too stubborn to listen to anybody. Look at me, the entire Ministry, the entire state listens to me, but my own son, refuses to." He was getting even more agitated. "Give me one good reason, one purpose in your life that you seek here. If any of your reasons have any strength of argument, I won't stand in your way, but unless you can do so, you are answerable to me. After all, I did not raise you to see you waste your life."

"This is not wasting father."

"Then what is it?"

Barin was silent.

"Are you in love with Malati?" His father stood up and looked out of window.

27

He did not answer and looked the other way.

"Answer my question." His father insisted in a tremulous voice.

"Yes I am."

"Unbelievable, you are in love with a rustic and illiterate mother of a child."

"So you wont stop pushing me until you make me talk, would you?"

"You got me right."

"Yes you are a politician."

"If your stay were for fun or vacation, I won't have any objections, but a decision which affects your mother and me, sure does concern me."

"In October 1942 you were deployed with the British forces."

"October 1942. This is no time for stories Barin. I should have been in the ministerial meeting today, not having this talk with you."

"I never asked you to come."

"Yes you never did, that is the problem. The problem with me is that I am your father."

"Tell me something. How many kinds of families are possible in this world?"

"What is that question supposed to mean?"

"In October 1942 you were deployed at Rajhat village, in Orissa. There had been a drought. Instead of sending you overseas to battle with allies, you were kept back."

"How did you know all this?"

"You also made hand bombs and bombed Captain Roddick's home."

His father looked at him eagerly.

"Captain Roddick was taken to the hospital later, but he died. He was survived by his newly married wife. You fled the town but came back when you came to know that nobody suspected that you did it. You went back to Captain Roddick's house."

Barin's father, who was standing close to the window, walked to him and pulled a chair.

"You got closer to Mrs. Roddick and expressed your deep feeling of sympathy for her. You asked her to go back to England but she refused. You came closer to her and visited here everytime you went to Bhubaneshwar. Meanwhile, you got married to mother."

His father was staring at him. He was looking as if a deep rooted secret, a secret buried somewhere deep inside the earth had suddenly been unearthed, and kept in front of him as a surprise. He was least ready for it.

"What happened to Mrs Roddick after that father?"

His father was silent. Moved with frailty and arrested in emotions of trust and distrust of a moment, which he had perhaps left far behind himself. His anger and agitation had evaporated in the small room full of slime and dung. But memories, however far behind one leaves them, come back with the slightest tingling, bringing back the same fervor and taste and distaste along with it.

Malati was standing at the door.

"What happened Malati?" Barin walked to her.

"I send Tiku to ask you if you need anything, but I don't know where he disappeared. May be those brats have got together again."

"Come in."

She walked in.

"He is my father."

"So Tiku is your son." His father turned his head to look at her

29

but the next words got gagged in his mouth. He stared at her.

"What happened babu?"

"Have been living here since your childhood?"

"Yes, after I was adopted by the landlord here when I was very small, I have been living here ever since."

"What happened to the landlord?"

"What could happen to him? He died of some disease. What else could happen to him if he would sleep with so many women?"

The father stared at her. She bore such a close resemblance to somebody he had known intimately. He did not dare to ask her anything else but he was sure that he had picked up a broken thread. Her unusually fair skin, the striking resemblance to Mrs. Roddick is what he could not drive off his mind. He sat silently next to Barin in the back seat of his car during the journey home to Calcutta. He never talked to Barin about the village or his future. His fatherliness was consumed by the memory of the moment when a daughter was born to Elaine Cooper Roddick, to whom he was a father too.

I could tell that the story had caught Rimi is attention. Ravi was ready to throw an opinion.

"Where is the kid Tiku now?"

"I don't know about that. I will have to go and look for him one of these days."

"When did it happen?"

"I guess somewhere in the eighties."

"Where is your uncle now?"

"He passed away last year. He had contacted some acute infection. He refused to get to a city hospital."

"Why would he refuse to get hospitalized?"

"He thought that life should be left to run its natural course; any external aid contaminates the idea of a life cycle."

"The village must have had a clinic too." Ravi contemplated.

"I don't know about that. But the interesting thing is that he has left his huge diary with me. He was an amazing writer. You guys will get to hear more his fables."

"Hey look, Richa is here." Rimi stood up when she saw the yellow Santro pulling in.

4

Richa, Rimi's cousin and the drive to the jungle

If words could define Richa they would plainly say, blonde. Five feet five, dyed hair, Versace glasses, branded from head to toe.

'Why Santro, then?' I thought I would ask when the time comes.

"Look at those heels." Ravi noticed, while the two girls threw themselves at each other, hugging, squeezing.

"This will be fun."

The squeeze was getting harder and harder I guess. The happy embraces turned into squeals. One of them lifted the other in the air. That was one happy meet. The release orders came by when a car behind the Santro honked. The Santro stood right in the driveway. Richa did her girl walk back to her car, throwing her hands to and fro to her sides. She quickly pulled it up into an empty spot.

"Boss Ravi. Are you thinking what I am thinking?"

"I think so." Ravi looked at me, and we were in accordance.

Ruchi came out again. Her Jeans fit tightly over her hips and thighs revealing her shape. Her black 'bebe' top failed to cover her navel, even when stretched to its very end. The stomach on display highlighted some muscles. For a second I thought I would have loved to see a piercing in her navel, and just observe the looks in Ravi's eyes.

"Do you think a piercing would have looked better?" I asked Ravi.

"In her navel?" He leaned over me, while we both stood next to our back packs.

"Where else?"

"Her nose."

"I haven't reached there yet."

"Her navel. It might have looked good."

"Since when have you started liking piercing?"

"These days you expect it with the kind of her bearings."

"Ya true. If she were Ravi's daughter, he would rush her to the tattoo master."

"Did you see that? She actually has a tattoo on her back." Ravi was leching.

Richa had turned around by then. Some tattoo marked her back, just above her hips.

"Somebody has done some good work on her." Ravi exclaimed.

I won't say that I did not like her. She was hot. But I knew better how not to let my eyes pop out, unlike Ravi. It's his basic instincts I guess. I however knew he would be back to normal, showing his usual generosity. Marriage I guess posts a lot of hunger on famished faces. I noticed Richa's firm breasts. I could bet a thousand that she was wearing one of those padded bras. Then I noticed her husky voice.

"Hey Dev, Ravi. I am sorry for making you wait for so long.

My grandmother was using my rest room and I had to wait for her for over almost half an hour." Richa confessed like a child.

"You could have used the other ones Ruchi." Rimi shot back.

"All my stuff, the girly stuff, was in that one. I had to wait."

"Hey, never mind. We are not that late yet." I attempted to ease the moment.

"Is that your luggage?" I saw her drag the wheeled suitcase.

"Yes. Richa told me that we were supposed to carry back packs, but since I don't have one, I got this." She sweetly responded, unable to comprehend the need.

"Alright, but I think you will be more comfortable in sneakers instead." I tried.

"No, I am absolutely fine. They are my favorites."

"Richa, what Dev is trying to say is that on our trip, you would find sneakers more comfortable. Moreover you won't find a lot of guys around to stare at you any ways." Rimi explained.

"Oh." Richa sighed.

"Ya. Consider we two the best you can have for the next two days." Ravi smiled in his magic attitude.

Richa had the deep concern on her face.

"What happened?" Ravi asked.

"I haven't got my sneakers."

"Alright, let's forget it."

"I can go back home real quick and get them."

"No." I, Ravi and Rimi stopped her in chorus.

"May be we can pick a pair up on our way." I tried to fake a smile.

Richa gave some blank looks. Then suddenly she had a flash of glee on her face. I understood what she meant. I felt foolish upon letting the girl prospect about shopping. I could see the backpacking trip falling flat on its face.

"Guys I forgot. I am Richa."

We pronounced our own names yet again. Ravi finally got rid of the itch in his palms. He shook hands and entered the first communication of comfort. It was an obvious pairing. I could hardly ever think of managing Richa. She was too flamboyant for me, even for a talk over the table. I would get too confused. I would lose the ends.

"Where are we guys heading, if I may ask?" Richa asked.

She had the habit of throwing her shoulder length hair sideways. She always talked with the side of her face towards one, with the hair always swept to the other side. I thought she was exercising her neck well. I would have really wanted to take her on a real back country trip where she would run out of all hair creams and lotions. I wonder what she would do then. I remembered the spoilt girl from the series 'Lost'. Even upon being lost she was hardly ready to believe that she was lost. I don't know if the comparison went well. Perhaps Richa would adjust soon. But those are the moments when a man's nerves are put to some real test. I thought for a moment whether she wondered what was going on in my mind. I wondered whether she was even remotely aware about what was going to come upon her, in a short time.

"We are going to a remote jungle."

"Wow. That is a surprise." Rimi remarked.

"What happened to that village of your, what did you say the name is, yes Chundi?" Ravi asked quickly.

"Change of plans to accommodate the new members." I wondered if such a village even existed.

"And how exactly are we going?"

"See that black Pathfinder?" I pointed to the black SUV parked across the street. Everyone looked at it. "That would be our baby for the ride."

"When did you get that?" Ravi asked.

"I did not, I borrowed it."

"I am excited. I have never been to a forest before." Richa flooded us with her enthusiasm. I saw her do a few small skips.

"You will now." I reassured her. "How about you Rimi? Are you ok with the idea?"

"Sure Sir. Whatever the boss decides."

"There you go; I have got a nice team I should say." My thoughts went to Richa as I thought. "Have I really?"

"But would we have place to stay?" Richa asked.

"Yup, I know the guest house people at Chitua. Not a problem." I replied.

"You planned it long time back, right?" I saw Ravi staring hard at me.

"What?"

"This forest thing?"

"Not at all. I was all for going to a village. But then it might not be possible for us to do a back country thing. I think it's better to go the reserve forest, take elephant rides and have fun for the two next days."

"Elephant ride. I did that once in Kerela." Richa got the shot of enthusiasm again. "When I was small this elephant blessed me and that I got a ride on its back."

"When did you go to Kerela?" Rimi asked her cousin.

"We went there on one of dad's tours. I was pretty small

though. That's all I remember and that too because we have the pictures at home. And you know what, the elephant farted and farted and kept farting. When I thought it has done enough, it released a huge load of dung." She looked at everybody, expecting laughs. Realizing that it wasn't funny enough she further added. "And it smelled like elephant shit." Her face turned innocent.

That time everybody smiled.

"How long will it take?" Ravi asked.

"Around six hours, in that truck" I said as I led them. "We will pick up a bag for Richa on our way. She needs a back pack and a pair of sneakers."

"But why does she need a back pack?" Ravi asked. "I don't think we are allowed to carry our packs on elephants."

"We will take a guided tour, we will trek."

"Trek in the jungle? Are you mad?"

"I said a guided tour, with a professional."

"Have you ever done that before?"

"Yes, lot of times."

"I don't trust you." Ravi felt a little uneasy.

"You shouldn't feel scared of this forest. The one you should really feel scared of, is Sundarbans."

"What's so special about this one? Does it have a name? Does it have tigers?"

"This forest is called Panida. There are hardly any tigers left there. Sundarbans is still pretty much natural. The marshes and bays and the dwellers are still those native to that place. There is a harmony, but even they don't wander deep inside. And if you are a visitor, forget it. The tiger knows well that you don't know your way out. It won't kill to eat you, but just for the fact that you are an intruder. Stay calm, it doesn't touch you, but how many people can stay calm at the sight of a tiger?"

"You are saying as if you have had the experience."

"Yes, I have."

Ravi stared at me through the corner of his eyes. It betrayed skepticism.

"See, this is why I like a Pathfinder; ample space." I opened the back door, thrust the entire luggage in.

"You have a bike rack too here," Rimi asked as she held the bike rack over the spare wheel.

"You should come with me someday; its fun." I smiled back at Rimi.

"I get to sit in the front." Richa quicky opened the passenger side door and threw herself in. Every body else followed. I went behind the wheels. Ravi and Rimi got in the back seats.

"You have to navigate."

"Directions?"

"We take Forty Seven North and then Twenty West." I said.

It worried Richa.

"Don't worry I know the way. Just watch out when I am feeling sleepy." I took the worry off her head.

"Should I shake you up then?"

"No, just open the door and jump out. Let this guy fall in the ditch or valley, alone. I am sure we will run through valleys." Ravi gave a thought.

"Oh yes; lots of valleys. It's a beautiful drive."

"I will so very love it." Richa grinned like a chestire cat as she pulled the sun shade down and checked herself out.

"Are you guys comfy?" I looked back to check if Rimi and Ravi were comfortable.

"Can't be, as long as you are driving." Ravi expressed his concern.

I adjusted my seat and the steering. I pushed the beast on the first gear and we took off.

"What about his driving?" Rimi asked.

"This guy; he has a history of falling asleep while driving. When he drives, everybody else has to stay awake. Ha ha ha."

"I am sure he is better than that." Rimi came to rescue me.

"Alright, you will see. I am getting my belts on." Ravi braced himself to safety.

"Richa you too." I asked Richa to belt herself.

I pulled down the window on my side. Richa was playing some punk music that I hardly understood. In half an hour, Richa was asleep. I lowered the volume to the music.

"Are you guys doing alright back there?" I asked, half turning my head, though I couldn't see them directly.

"Yes we are." Rimi replied.

"What is Ravi doing?" I adjusted the rear view mirror so I could see Rimi.

She looked at me directly at first. Then she realized that I was better visible in the mirror. I smiled at her.

"Guess, he is asleep." She looked at Ravi.

"Are his eyes half closed?" I asked.

"Can't see from here."

"Look closely."

She raised herself to bend directly over his eyes.

"I guess they are half closed." She moved back to her seat. She pulled the soft toy tiger cub from the back. I saw her pull it in her lap.

"That is Simba; my pet." I was watching her in the mirror.

"Simba; isn't that the cub from the Lion King?"

I shook my head.

"Yes, and when he grew up he had a beautiful girl friend." Ravi mumbled.

I smiled, aware that Ravi wasn't asleep. Richa was snoring by then.

"See now who all are sleeping. My navigator is dreaming merrily." I said.

"She wants to get there before we do." Ravi mumbled back.

How I wished that Ravi could fall asleep too. At least he didn't know about the secret of the rear view mirror.

"I think you need to adjust the rear view mirror. There is a lot of traffic behind us." Ravi spoke in sleepy voice.

I was convinced that Ravi was faking that voice. He was perfectly awake. I adjusted the mirror again.

"Ravi, why don't you drive? I have been driving for long."

Ravi snuggled back into his sleepy position. Something woke Richa up. She sat all awake, as if she had never slept.

"What happened? Did you see a snake?"

"How did you know? I just dreamt that I was in a cave full of snakes. A lot of cavemen were grilling a boar." Richa was sweating.

"What were you doing?" I teased her.

"I was tied to a pole and gagged."

"Gagged?" I wondered. "The cavemen were advanced enough. What did they gag you with?"

"I don't know." Richa certainly had that innocence in her. I stopped teasing her further.

"Can I sit in the back, when we stop next? I want to sit next to Rimi."

"Yeah sure. We will stop and take a five minute break. You girls might want to get fresh. We still have two hours before we reach."

"How about getting lunch too?" Richa's voice was mauled by her yawn.

"Not a bad idea, a little early though. A dhaba?"

"As if you will find a rated French cuisine on the way." Ravi kept shooting around the corner. He had half sunk in the comfort of the seat and gone down as far as his belt could let him.

"Then Rimi will tell us a story."

"What story?" Rimi smiled in surprise.

"Any thing. It's lunch time so a story about some kind of lunch would be fine."

"But I don't know any."

"I know you read a lot of Reader's Digest ways. Don't tell me you can't come up with a single story."

"But I am not a story teller."

"Well you can try. How will you survive when you have kids."

"When we have kids." Ravi mumbled.

"What?" I asked, pretending I hadn't heard him.

"Nothing, carry on." Ravi replied.

"Think of something meanwhile." I encouraged Rimi

"Let me try." Rimi had a doubt on her face.

We pulled over for some gas. We spotted a *dhaba* next to it. Richa couldn't hold her hunger and neither could I. Ravi's sleep was broken by the spice and chilly in the *dal*. He rushed to the restroom to look for some cold water. He came back as fast as he went. The water was as hot as a freshly boiled pot of porridge. He quenched himself with a chilled bottle of beer. That's the only thing cold the place had. Rimi had her meal peacefully. I was observing her very closely and at the same time each and every action of her was attracting me towards her. Fortunately we found a store next door that dealt in accessories. Richa had to do with a cheap back pack we found and a pair of military sneakers. The part boot, part sneakers, seemed to be heavier than her feet. She could hardly lift her foot up at first. I was reminded of the robot cop and congratulated her for her re-enactment of the role. I was glad that she found it funny.

"But how would you run if a tiger chases you?" I teased her.

"The first thing I will do is to take these shoes off and throw them at his face. I bet this will break his strongest canine."

So true, I thought. I thanked the lord that tigers don't have a mane, else Richa would know what to do with it.

Ravi purchased half a dozen beer bottles for the journey.

"Any thing you girls want to drink?" I asked.

"I will get a Pepsi." Richa seemed to know what she wanted.

"Any thing for you Rimi?"

"I am fine. I have water with me."

"And I have a pack of it in the car."

We set sail again.

"Rimi." I looked at her in a quick flash. "Your story."

"I am still thinking."

"Let us know when you are ready."

"I will tell you a true incident. It happened to my friend Jini." Rimi volunteered after a moment's silence.

"Did you say Jini as in Jini?" I spelled the name.

"Yes, her name is Jini."

"Coincidence right. You are only two syllables different from her."

Rimi smiled back.

"Alright tell us." I told her to begin.

5

Ripples in Jini's life

"Something is falling."

"I don't see anything."

"Trust me, I see something."

"Why don't I see anything?"

"Watch carefully." Kabir pointed out. "Look, there."

"Either I am blind, or you are playing a prank." Jini tried to look more carefully.

"What do you expect me to do?"

"At least try helping me."

"Alright, concentrate at this point. Try it all over again."

Both were looking at a stereogram. Kabir was a student in molecular biology. He could see all such pictures at the first sight. It was difficult for Jini though. She worked for the radio. She was good at speaking. The moment it came to scrutinizing, she held her hands high up, acknowledging defeat. They had met first a few days back at Saket Community Centre. The radio channel was on a promotion drive. Jini noticed the big eyed guy throwing glances at her. It wasn't the first time that such a thing had happened, but it was that accidental moment that made it a clincher. Kabir was standing in a corner, watching Jini speak into the microphone. Lost in the gaze, he did not notice the cow aiming straight for him. Saket is not known for such mishaps, but somehow this cow had appeared from nowhere. It headed straight for Kabir, ending in a huge collision. The cow must have been unaware of the impact, but Kabir later thanked the gods for leaving the animal without horns. Blown off the spot, Kabir landed at the pulpit, just below the dais where Jini was trying to address the audience. She was actually requesting for a volunteer, and he at the right moment, landed right at the spot, bingo. The crowd was scattered. Jini did not know what to do. She got down and made for Kabir.

"How are you feeling, sir?"

Kabir looked up once at her, and let his head rest on the concrete. He was knocked out. The crowd carried him to a corner. Jini got disturbed, she couldn't proceed. She handed over the microphone to her substitute. The sun winked for a second. The clouds appeared from nowhere. As the substitute took over, things started getting back to normal. Kabir's moans were not to be ignored. As a mark of good gesture, Jini went to the hospital with him. Kabir was rushed to the ICU.

"Doctor, is he alright now?" Jini asked the doctor.

"He looks alright. It might take some time heal though. It seems it was a big impact. Did you actually see it happen?"

"Yes, I did."

"Are you his err…" The doctor examined her. "Girlfriend?"

"Well, yes and no." She did not know what to say. She thought that she must relay the event on radio, once the gentleman recovered. People would definitely find it funny and moreover such good gestures always added to ones kitty.

"Alright, are his parents around?"

"I tried…"

"He is a lucky guy. Not many people are left in one piece after such a blow. Well we have something for you to do." The doctor did not wait for her to finish her sentence.

"What is that?"

"Be around him. He might need you."

"Alright doc." Jini responded, not knowing what else she should be doing.

Having obtained the title of being Kabir's girlfriend, she could go inside the patient's room. Kabir had been moved to the regular ward. She knocked once and walked in. Kabir was lying on a reclining bed. He did not look that bad under the covers, but the doctor said that his lower back had to be plastered all the way. She went close to him. He seemed to be asleep. She stared at him, he did have baby cheeks. She felt a soft tickle for him. She scanned him from head to toe. His hands were on his sides. She checked for wedding rings. None. She felt elated for a moment. His chin bore a strange scar. A cut, perhaps, something had happened years back. She felt a strong urge to kiss him. His eyes were closed, and she could. That shouldn't have woken him up. She gently moved her lips close to his and planted a noiseless kiss. It did feel good. Sometimes a kiss is a healer, but that time, it was different. An old picture hanging on the wall, next to the bed fell down. The glass crashed into pieces. It took her by surprise. She quickly rose and picked the picture up. A middle aged woman draped in shawls with a puppy peeking out. The woman looked poor, the puppy was unconcerned. Her looks were like an Afghani woman. She liked the picture. The nurse came in, perhaps startled by the noise.

"What happened?"

"Oh nothing, the picture suddenly fell down?"

"What picture?" She then saw all the shattered glass. "Oh my god. Are you hurt?"

"No, not at all. The nail might have been loose. It fell by itself."

"Oh, these people. How poorly they do the things." She made a wild face at the picture Jini was holding. "Let me call for help."

Jini held on to the picture. She thought that she would keep it, if nobody asked her to give it back. Help came in a few minutes. An old maid came in with a duster and trough. She squatted and started sweeping the spot.

"Aahh..." The old maid winced.

"What happened?" Jini turned to look at her.

"I cut myself."

"Oh, let me see." Jini looked at her palms. Blood was gushing out. "Gosh. Let me call for help." She rushed out and dragged the first nurse she found. "The maid has cut herself badly. You need to come with me."

"What happened?"

"She cut herself, while cleaning the glass on the floor."

"What glass?"

"Please come with me, she is bleeding badly."

The nurse followed her. They entered the room to find the maid holding her right palm with her left and pressing hard against it. The nurse opened the first aid box, pulled out a bunch of liquids and dressings. The maid was feeling ok in the next ten minutes. The floor looked a little bloody though.

"You should go home today. With your age and the amount of blood you have lost, you need to take a break and recover." The nurse dictated.

The maid shook her head. She bent over to pick up the trough with the broken pieces of glass.

"Let it be. I will ask somebody else to do it." The nurse said.

The maid shook her head again and went away.

"Who is treating this patient?" The nurse asked.

"I think it's Doctor Kailash". Jini had to close her eyes and imagine the doctor wearing his crest.

"Alright, I will send for Sister Rebecca." She went to the foot board and picked up the patient's papers.

Jini sat on the chair for a few seconds, gazing at Kabir's face. She wondered where he came from. She looked at the window. The large french window invited a lot of light in. She walked to it. She looked out at the streets. She saw a lot of traffic and imagined a lot of noise. The traffic however appeared not to be moving. The streets looked jammed. She ran her eyes as far as she could. She saw a huge crowd. In the meantime sister Rebecca had come in. She examined the patient's papers again and readjusted the I-V. Jini noticed her.

"What has happened Sister?"

"Where?"

"Out there. I see a huge crowd."

Sister stood next to her and looked out. "A huge tree has fallen, it has blocked the traffic."

"Oh dear!"

"I heard someone say that it was the tallest tree around. The biggest problem is for the ambulances that tow patients. We are using the back doors of the building today." She turned to look at Jini directly. "Is somebody else coming for the patient, or will you be the only one around?"

"Well, I..."

"Are you his girlfriend?"

"Aaa..."

"Alright, doctor Kailash said that the patient can be moved tomorrow. You will need to go downstairs and sign all his release papers. Did you already take care of the insurance stuff?"

"Yes, I did." Jini remembered having signed the papers and charge it to her credit card. She did not know about Kabir's papers. Moreover, his name was the only thing they could find in his wallet. His driving license had an address, but she hadn't made any inquiries yet. His cell phone seemed to be dead. Bottom line she had not been able to inform anybody who knew him. Everything had happened so fast. She looked at his face again. Indeed, everything was happening so fast.

"The doctor would be here after an hour." The nurse went out.

Jini went to the window again. She saw the traffic getting denser each moment. She went back to the chair, dragged it close to Kabir. She supported her chin on her palms, resting her elbows on the bed. She got the best view of his face. She seemed to be getting attracted in by his looks. She herself wasn't a beauty, but she was pretty, better than most, any day. She looked at his nose. It had the perfect shape. It rose from his forehead and came down straight. It did not have any curves. It was almost perfect; his skin and long face. Her phone rang.

"Hey Mansi."

"Where are you?"

"At the hospital."

"What are you doing at a hospital? Kumar sir is mad at you. You need to come over right away."

"I am with a patient here. I can't come right now."

"Somebody I know?"

"No you don't. Even I don't know him."

"Is the patient serious?"

"Not any longer. He is sleeping now."

"Alright, so he is alright now." Mansi stressed on the word 'He'.

"Ya, but I have to stay around. None of his folks are here yet."

"You will get in trouble someday for your softy-softy heart. By the way is that the same guy at the show in the morning?"

"Ah, so people know."

"Oh yes, everybody is laughing. I think a cow horned his bottom. He must look more horny now."

"Stop being funny. He was hurt,."

"Did you check it, yourself?" Mansi again stressed on the word 'yourself'

"Forget it. Tell me, how the show ended in the morning?"

"Do you really want to know?"

"Why yes. How did Kiran do?"

"Well, Kumar fired her."

"Fired, why?"

"Don't ask why. People can be assholes sometimes."

"By people you mean Kumar."

"Who else?"

"Huh"

"What do you want me to tell him?"

"Tell him this is an emergency, can't leave the patient. And don't relate any 'he she' issue."

"Alright, so long."

Jini saw Kabir twisting and cringing.

"Hey, I will call you back later."

"Ok, later."

She hung up. Kabir opened his eyes and saw Jini sitting there. He opened and shut and eyes a number of times, unable to believe what he was seeing. It was like nothing had happened since the morning. He started right where he left, watching Jini.

"How are you feeling now?"

"It's painful. I can't move."

"I think it will take a couple of days to get better."

"Shit!"

"What happened?"

"My final semester exams. If I miss them I will waste a year. Oh shit shit shit." Kabir stared at himself. He tried harder to move, just to verify whether it was for real. He groaned, looked agitated, while Jini watched with pity. In a while, he gave up. He accepted the fact he would not be able to move for some time.

"What kind of exam is that?" Jini asked.

"Final year MBBS, AIIMS."

"Oh, you yourself are a doctor."

"Not one, yet and maybe not for another year. But why did this have to happen?"

"It sure is unfortunate." Jini pursed her lips.

Kabir looked at Jini, then looked away. In spite of his acute pain, her looks were dazzling him. His thoughts wandered from his predicament to his feelings for her. He grew calmer.

"Thanks"

"For what?"

"For being here with me. If you were not here, you would have been at work, right?"

"Yes." Jini shook her head.

Kabir looked at Jini again. That time their eyes met each other. Jini reclined on her chair. She looked down.

The nurse came in with a tray in her hands.

"How is the patient doing now?"

"I think alright." Jini replied.

"I am asking the patient." The nurse corrected Jini.

"It's paining real bad." Kabir groaned a little, as his thoughts wandered back to his pain.

"It will for a while. I will give another set of medicines and a shot. I hope you are not scared of shots."

"Who isn't?"

She set the tray down and helped Kabir take the medicines. Next, she prepared the shots. Jini stood next to him. Kabir closed his eyes, anticipating the pain. Jini noticed his concern. She held Kabir's hands. While the nurse gave the shot, two palms pressed tightly against each other.

"What do you do?" The nurse asked Kabir, trying to engage him in talks.

"AIIMS, MBBS, final year." Kabir said with a broken voice, without any interest, just because he had been asked.

"Ah, so you yourself are a doctor."

Kabir looked dizzier.

"I expected a volley of questions from you."

"Why?" Kabir asked back.

"Earlier experience with docs. They always think they know better than any body else."

Kabir smiled at Jini.

"I would like to meet my doctor."

"Who, Doctor Kailash?"

"Yes."

"Well, you will be treated by doctor Sharma now."

"Why?"

"His daughter met with an accident today."

"Oh. How is she now?"

"No word yet. Doctor Sharma will come by soon. You can sleep, if you do feel sleepy."

"Yeah, I am feeling dizzy."

The nurse left with her tray.

Jini and Kabir had a new frontier to deal with. Both held hands. She felt like kissing him again. His eyes closed. She kissed him on his lips again. Kabir's lips parted, trying best to kiss back. He least wanted to be knocked out, and at such a moment.

Jini paced around in the room. He was to be a doctor, that too from AIIMS. It rang the sweet bells of happiness in her head. She could only wish that he wasn't going around with any body else. How she wanted to talk to him desperately. She felt restless. She was waiting for him to wake up. All the broken glasses had been cleared up. Doctor Sharma came in the next hour. He examined the papers. He checked the patient with his stethoscope. Kabir woke up. He rubbed his eyes.

"Are you feeling ok now?"

"Me." Kabir responded with a drowsy voice. He was still asleep, technically.

"The nurse told me you go to AIIMS."

Kabir nodded.

Jini stopped pacing and sat back on the chair. She so wanted Kabir to get well soon.

"How is Dr. Kailash's daughter?" Kabir asked.

"His daughter, I think is fine now." Dr. Kumar smiled as he looked at Kabir.

"Is she in this hospital?" Jini asked.

"No, she is at Escorts. So you are his girlfriend. The entire hospital knows now."

"What?"

"Are you not Jini Chabbria? The radio jockey?"

"Yes I am." She remembered signing her name downstairs. Somebody even asked her if she was the same Jini.

"What was that tag line of yours? 'Yours Truly Jini'. My kids are mad about you."

Jini smiled, half shy, half thrilled.

"You need to take care of this guy real well now." He addressed Jini. "And you, lucky guy. You have made a nice steal." He winked at Kabir. "Don't try getting naughty for the next few days."

The doctor left. Another maid came in and hung another framed picture on the same spot where the nail was still on the wall. Jini looked at the table, to check if the old picture was still there. She rose to help the maid put the picture up. This picture had a magnified view of circular ripples in water and a finger touching the centre, the source of the disturbance. She occupied the chair again. Kabir stared at the picture. He then stared back at Jini.

"Can you come closer?"

Jini moved closer.

"Why are we here?" Kabir asked.

"Well, you met with an accident…"

"No, but why exactly did everything happen?" Kabir cut her short. "With you sitting next to me, I don't seem to feel the pain. Your presence seems to be the biggest healer."

Jini looked at him, her eyes full of warmth.

Kabir was released the next day. Jini asked Kabir to move in with her, when she came to know that he was on his own. Jini assisted him in doing his daily chores. They grew very close. Ten days later Kabir felt stronger, he however couldn't walk without assistance. They were working out the stereogram in the evening.

"Something is falling."

"I don't see anything."

"Trust me, I see something."

"Why don't I see anything?"

"Watch carefully." Kabir pointed out. "Look, there."

"Either I am blind, or you are playing a prank." Jini tried to look more carefully.

"What do you expect me to do?"

"At least try helping me." "Alright, concentrate at this point. Try it all over again."

Jini did concentrate. She saw a picture in three dimensions. A ripple of disturbance in water, a finger touching the eye of the disturbance.

"I see it now."

"Do you remember such a picture?"

"Why yes, there was a similar picture in the hospital ward." Jini knitted her brows.

"We have talked about everything that happened, so many times. The picture frame shattering, the maid cutting her hands, the traffic jam, your friend being fired from her job, Dr. Kailash's dauther meeting with an accident. Do you think there is a connection?"

"What kind of connection?"

"The world trying to adjust to our relationship."

Jini stared at him.

"And all the ripples were left by that finger, me staring at you at the show. I forgot the world around me. I could have been careful."

"And are they living happily ever after?" I asked as I quickly clapped, juggling my hands on the wheels.

"Pretty much."

"I would really like to meet the couple."

Rimi just laughed. We were past Jamnagar and read the gates that announced, 'Welcome to Panida National Park'.

The security guards checked the car real quick and let us in after I showed them a letter.

"So you also had a letter." Ravi commented.

I just nod my head.

"You knew we are coming here. You liar."

"I just had that letter for a while." I showed him the dates. He read the contents which entitled me to enter the park any time in the year 2002. It was signed by the IFO at the park.

"But why did you keep it with you in the first place? I did not see you go back in to get it."

"I had it with me, that's why I did not go back in." I was getting a little tired of Ravi's queries.

We drove through the terrain. I felt the pride of driving the pathfinder.

"So you know the way in?" Ravi asked.

"By my heart. Morever, they have signs all around."

I kept driving for an hour.

"It's so beautiful outside." Richa was jumping on her seat.

"That is true."

"When will we reach the guest house?" She asked.

"We are very close."

I took a deliberate turn inside the jungle when nobody was noticing. The terrain had become more uneven. It was tough jungle tracks, not used very often. Richa kept appreciating the beauty.

"Look out, a bear." She pointed out towards an old log of wood in excitement. Though, I swear that it did look like a bear.

We drove close to the log. I went out and felt the log with my fingers. I rubbed some loose dust of dead wood. Then I walked back to the passenger door. I asked Richa to lower her window. She tried opening the door, but I shut it back and gestured her to sit inside.

"Watch your bear for real." I whispered.

"But that is just a log of wood." She shouted back.

"Hush. Not your bear. Look over there, beyond those bushes." I pointed out to a spot about a hundred yards from us. It was open grass lands, but at the far end stood a lone leopard.

Richa looked at it through dazzled dazzling eyes. Rimi joined her from behind her window.

"Wake Ravi up, he is missing a scene."

Rimi woke the sleeping angel up.

"Son of a bitch. That's a real leopard." He stared at it. "What are we doing here? Let's go. What if it comes for us?"

"Don't worry it won't." I kept standing next to the door.

Suddenly the leopard seemed to notice us. It looked our way and took a few steps. Then it sat down and licked its paws.

"I am scared." Richa acknowledged.

"Shh…" I hushed her again.

I got back in the car and purred the car back to life.

"Let's get closer to it." I announced.

"We are not going any closer." Ravi stood up the back seat, his foot over the bridge between the front seats as he held the steering tight.

"Don't be a kid. It won't do anything. We will sit inside. Trust me I have done this before."

"No we are not going."

"Will you sit back and relax. And let's talk softly. We don't want to disturb the animals around."

"Precisely; the reason why we should leave the leopard alone."

"Alright, let's get a little further at least."

Ravi let the wheels loose. I kept driving the SUV closer and closer. I knew what a safe distance is.

"Stop the vehicle now." Ravi seemed to be very agitated.

"Don't worry, just sit and relax."

The terrain was a narrow path, barely enough for a vehicle.

"Relax. How the hell can I fucking relax? You are leading us straight into the mouth of a beast."

"I know how it works, just be patient."

"Patience, my ass." He stood up again and this time he held the steering and forced a turn. The car swung wildly. I lost control and heard a small desperate squeal which sounded like Rimi's voice and the SUV had already banged into a pile of rocks. I got back to senses after a minute of concussion. I realized that the

SUV sat right across the path, the front part elevated in the air, at an angle to the horizontal.

"Are you alright?" I heard the others saying.

I felt blood trickle down my forehead. I thought that I could rescue the vehicle. It was an all wheel drive. The engine however seemed to be dead. I tried to turn the ignition, but I couldn't get it back to life. I remembered that we were heading towards the leopard. I looked out of the window. I had expected the leopard either to ignore the situation or run away. Incidentally, I saw it walking towards us.

"I can't turn it on. We will have to go out and pull it back on track." I analyzed. "And why the hell did you have to do that Ravi." I was angry enough at him. Perhaps I should have realized that I was with others and considered everyone before taking a decision.

The girls were stunned into silence.

"The leopard is walking towards us." Richa noticed. She leaped towards me for assurance. Rimi shifted more towards Ravi, towards her left. The leopard was approaching the wreck from the right.

"We will wait for it to inspect, and leave. And nobody here acts funny. Just close your eyes and sit back. Richa, go back and lie straight on the floor, near Rimi's feet. You need not even move." I turned to look at Ravi. "Ravi please co-operate this time. We are in a mess and you must act as I say."

The animal was getting closer and closer.

"Listen, if you guys don't act funny, it won't be attracted a lot to what is inside. It might not even notice the glass windows. It will do a search, and just leave. But again, no body must move. Drop dead and lock the doors. Here I will lock them." I pushed the central lock down.

Everybody did as I said. I took a position so I could see the animal through the parting of my lids. The leopard came close. It raised its front paws and rested them against the back windows. It looked in. It went around the car. It sniffed the sides. I guess it smelled the piss of dogs. It was rubbing itself hard against the wheels. I wondered why it did so. All the dried piss was from no leopard for sure. May be it was just curious. It came to the left side, jumped on the front bonnet, which usually is slanting when the car is on a flat road, but with the front end elevated, it was almost horizontal. It scratched the windshield with its claws. I could see the glass taking all the scratches. For a second I hated it. A wind shield cost a fortune. I was sure I could handle the leopard's curiousity, but was scared for the others. I could hear Richa breathe heavily. Her muffled squeaks were disturbing. The leopard sat erect, raising both its ears and watching intently. I was face to face with it. I was sitting straight, without any movement, no blinking. I could see it staring straight at me. Then it lay on its belly and hung its tongue out. It reached its nose closer to the wind shield. But it wasn't trying to see inside any longer. It was sniffing the glass. I wondered what made it throw a deal about the smell. Then I knew why it was doing so. It turned around, raised its tail and squirted a full load of pee. Had the glass not been there, it would have landed straight on my face. In a few moments I could smell it. It must have trickled inside and settled on the vents. It then jumped back down. It went to the right side and walked past the car, behind us. I took a breath of relief.

"Is it gone?" I heard the agitated voice of Rimi.

"Yes, you can open your eyes. But don't get up. Stay still." I adjusted the rear view mirror. I could see the animal walk away. "Don't you guys move; lie low."

I saw it climb a tree. I cursed myself and the damned leopard for not leaving. I hoped it wasn't planning to spend its evening there. I was right, it wasn't. It came down with a large kill. The leopard landed back on the ground, with something that looked like an antelope, gripping it by the neck. It walked idly. Then it made large leaps and in about ten strides it was back to our car again. It made a huge leap with the kill and made it straight over the roof. We could hear it panting. The roof creaked. A leopard could be heavy. I thought for a moment, what if we were in a Maruti? I put my fingers on my lips and looked back at my mates and made a strong gesture again to stay silent. I was keeping an eye on my watch. We could hear the thumps from the roof. The leopard might have been tearing the flesh off its kill. Ten minutes went by. Rimi tried peeking out of the window, towards the top, from where she was huddling. Suddenly a huge swing of something hit that side of the window. The leopard's tail. It ran across, from the top to the bottom. It was longer than that. It kept swinging. In no time I saw the first drop of blood trickling down my side of the window. I felt that if nothing else, this would surely drive these women crazy. I prayed that the roof could have a depression with the animal, and all the blood and carcass stay there. Suddenly I heard a thud and simultaneously a wild Ravi shriek. I closed my eyes tight. All motions from the roof had come to a stop. I smelled danger. I quickly looked back to inspect. The head of the antelope was dangling on Ravi's side. A pair of dead eyes were staring straight at him. The leopard resumed after the pause. I did not hear any birds. Monkeys somewhere far off were heaving. Amongst all the noise I distinguished one sound, hyena's laugh. I knew my mates hadn't noticed it, but I feared the worst.

6

We were not alone

I heard more laughs. Amongst all animals I feared hyenas the most. I heard the laugh coming from the left. I couldn't hear the monkeys any longer. The entire animal kingdom was scared of the wildest of the dog species. It did not respect privacy, it believed in snatching its meal.

"What is that strange sound?" Rimi asked. She had opened her eyes for a moment. I had silently reached back my arms, touched her hands and gestured her to close her eyes.

Ravi already looked pale. Richa kept herself in the pocket, around the floor. Best for her, I thought. I saw the first hyena. I had never seen one in the open before. I always wanted to have an encounter with them, but certainly not in this way. I preferred having professionals around me. But this was so different. I was responsible for four lives, three if I did not count mine. But I had to stay alive to save the others. I sensed my fear glands working, but I wasn't nervous. For a moment I thought what it would be like, being torn apart by a pack of those wild animals. It would just be a moment's pain. I would be in pieces, even before I would have noticed the pain. I abused myself for thinking like a fool. I knew as well as any body else did that wild did not attack humans, unless they were incited. We were not playing with them, were we? We were just silent spectators. What about the others though? How long could they hold out? It takes time to communicate or at least understand the language of the wild. They were new. It would be too easy to panic. The first hyena was standing at the edge of the bushes, right under a tree. It was standing side ways, its head towards us. I imagined the leopard on the roof staring straight at the animal. I held my hand back again, I held Rimi's hands. I looked back at them and gestured them to hold each other's hands. I saw all of them peeking out of the window. There was silence all around. I put my fingers on my lips again very strongly urging them to be absolutely quiet. I felt they were over the havoc of a leopard. They had accepted the fact. They understood that the leopard wasn't here for us. But could they hold on? The thumping resumed at the roof. The leopard was back at its meal. I wasn't praying for the carcass to stay on the roof any longer. I wanted the leopard to take the carcass down. The SUV might not be strong enough to carry the load of hyenas fighting for flesh. Moreover the rack was sharp enough to catch the bones. The entire carcass could never be removed. I saw a couple of more hyenas join the first one. They were approaching us. The numbers increased. We were stuck. We had to get out of the car. The hyenas were bound to make for the roof; their weight would bring it down. I could vouch that the windows would not stay intact after the maul. We were running short of time. I looked back at the others. The leopard seemed to be standing on the roof now. I could see its shadow on the ground. It was four thirty in the evening, looking at the sun and the shadow I presumed we were facing north. We would have to get out of the car. I won't have the map with me. We would have to leave all the stuff we carried. I felt good about the compass I had in my digital watch.

I could turn it on with a push of a button. I saw open fields to the right. It would take us deeper into the jungle. The dogs were to the left. I quickly made my calculations. As the hyenas approached, the leopard would guard its kill well. The first hyena would leap for the roof, may be from the bonnet end. The rest would surround the car. The leopard would then flee, to that nearest tree. We did not have more than a minute. I wondered why the hyenas were not running, usually they are supposed to. I watched closely, the paws looked immersed in the ground. Perhaps they were crossing a marsh. They knew the grounds better than I did. They knew what they were doing. It gave me a little more time, and I should be using it. I stopped my mind from getting distracted. I tried calculating the leopard's move. When we would have gone out of the wreck, the hyenas wouldn't have bothered us. But, what about the leopard? I quickly decided that we should get out of the car as soon as the hyenas were close enough. The leopard would get busy, and we could quickly run to the closest bush and sit there quietly. Thirty more seconds and we would have to make a move. The hyenas were picking up speed. The pack seemed to get larger every moment. I looked back quickly. In a low voice, I spoke with gestures.

"At the count of three everybody has to get out of the right door. We would run towards that bush and stay there. We are not going to run after that. We will have to wait till things settled down. No body panics. Everybody just look at that bush." Ravi was busy watching the hyenas. I thought I could hear his heart beats. "Ravi, we don't have time. Do as I say if you want to live." Everybody looked towards the bush. I opened the central lock. "All right at the count of three, Rimi, Richa, Ravi and then me." I was sure our movement would disturb the leopard above, but wanted to count on my experience.

"One, Two, Three." I counted faster than I should have. It was at the nick of time. The first hyena was a few yards from us. None of the guys were moving. I pushed the door open, and pushed Rimi out. I grabbed Richa and pushed her out. Ravi followed. We ran to the bush. It was just in time. I let the adrenalin settle down. The three of them huddled on me, behind me.

"Everybody, keep touching me." I ordered.

I saw the bunch of hyenas jump and scratch wildly. I heard the windows break. We had left the doors open. Some of them took turns to quickly inspect the inside and upon being disappointed that it did not lead to the roof, they came out. Two of them had their hind limbs on the bonnet, challenging the leopard directly. The cat was purring, not yet ready to leave. The entire car seemed to have disappeared under the dogs. The leopard made a clean leap off the SUV and made it for the tree. I felt a lot of sweat on me. I looked at my mates with reassuring eyes. The commotion was deafening. The hyenas could be irritable. I had never seen so many of them together. The animals pulled at the flesh. A side of the roof rack seemed to have opened up. The massive strength in the animals' jaws was stronger than the fasteners could bear. The sun was almost ready to disappear. We would have to spend the night, somewhere, somehow. In an hour the pack had finished the meal. The younger hyenas were having their turn. I could see a cage of bones on the SUV. The roof however still seemed to be intact.

"Guys, did any of you get a chance to check your cell phones?" I whispered.

Ravi fished in his pocket and took his phone out. He pressed a few buttons.

"No signal."

"I have a two way radio in the car. We will get back to the car as soon as the hyenas are gone."

"What about the leopard?" Rimi asked.

"It would have fled long back. Don't worry. It's no where around."

"Can we start the car again?" Ruchi asked.

"I don't know. We can try."

"It's entirely your fault. Why did you want to drive close to the leopard in the first place?" Richa spoke agitatedly.

"Animals are harmless Richa. I was just trying to give you guys a close view."

Richa slapped me hard and wept silently. I looked back at the hyenas making sure that we were not disturbing them. There was a sense of satisfaction in Ravi's eyes. He thought I deserved to be slapped. I did not look at Rimi. The hyenas were resting, rolling on the ground, chasing each other. One hyena came very close to our bush, with a piece of flesh in its jaws. Two more of them followed it. They fought over the flesh as they pulled at it from three different directions. In the commotion the piece landed, a couple of feet from us. The three of them leaped for it. They stopped when suddenly they saw us. I stared into the eyes of the largest one. I felt somebody's warm breath on my shoulders. It must have been Richa. I hoped that I had trained them enough to keep their mouth shut and not scream. The largest one made the first move. It inched closer and right next to the flesh, it squatted on the ground. We were looking at each other. I pushed my three mates back a little. I wanted them to understand that the animals needed a little more space. We moved back. The three animals pounced at the flesh again. They ran with whatever they got, away from the pack.

The commotion from the hyenas kept getting lower.

"Most of them are full and resting I guess. They won't stay here long, if they don't change their mind and decide to rest around." I told the rest.

"Look at that one." I pointed out at one of the animals. "She is the leader of the pack. See how the kids are all following her. I wish I had my camera here."

"The bastard wants his camera now." Ravi remarked. His voice seemed to be a little normal.

"Don't throw all faults on Dev." Rimi corrected Ravi in an angry mutter. "It was more of your fault. Why did you have to touch the steering? If Dev hadn't been here, we would have been dead by now."

Ravi and Rimi stared at each other and reached an understanding. I kept enjoying the sight of closeness to the wild.

"Are you guys alright now?" I asked.

Only Rimi shook her head. She was holding my arm tight.

"What do we do now?" She asked.

"Wait for them to clear out." I looked at the lazing hyenas.

"We go back to the car and try to salvage it." Ravi added.

The girls liked the idea. I had my own doubts about it though.

"Guys, I don't think we can use the car for the night. It's already starting to get dark. The car has fresh blood all over it. We have two options." I saw every body look at me intently. "We take all our stuff out and walk our way to the nearest settlement, or find the nearest watch tower and spend our nights there and come back to the car later in the morning."

"How are we going to find our way?" Ravi asked seriously.

"I have the maps."

"You have the maps too. When did you keep all that?"

"I don't think it's the right time to discuss all this."

"Who do you think you are?" Ravi held my collar in aggression and he squeezed my neck hard.

I stayed silent, did not want to increase the noise.

"Don't act like children boys." Rimi took him off me. "We have an issue here that needs to be resolved first. We can fight if we stay alive. For now I think Dev knows best what to do, let him make the decisions. Are you alright with that Richa?" She looked at her sister.

Richa nodded her head.

"And Ravi please..." Rini cried but never looked at Ravi.

7

The night falls

The wreck had cleared out. My watch showed eight. Richa was dozing in Rimi's lap. Ravi was sitting cross legged, his arms supporting his head.

"Look at the moon Rimi. We have a lot of light around." I addressed Rimi. I could see all her expressions. She was smiling.

"I will go and get the map, flash light and the radios." I continued.

She nodded her head. I held her hands.

"You are doing a good job Rimi." I kept looking at her.

"I will sponsor a night's drink at the Taj when we are back in Delhi." I brushed my fingers through Ravi's hair.

"Alright you guys wait here, like you are. No noise. I will go to the car and grab the stuff."

"Wait, I will go along with you." Ravi got up on his feet.

I felt better, but somehow did not feel comfortable leaving the girls alone.

"I have to pee." Rimi also got up and whispered in my ears.

"Nice timing, step a little away and use the bushes. Make sure that nobody bites your bottom." I warned her knowing that this wouldn't scare her.

She smiled.

"Why are you smiling?" I asked her. It was comforting to see her bold face.

"Shouldn't I be scared of the biggest animal standing next to me?"

"Wo, wo, wo… Are you suggesting something?"

"Go get the stuff." She sternly ordered.

"We will be a few minutes. Take care of your sister."

"I need to get some stuff too."

I looked back at her wondering what she wanted.

"Girly stuff." She replied.

I looked at the full moon and grunted.

"We don't want to pile up, alright. Ravi why don't I and Rimi go on this trip? You and Richa can go next." I suggested.

Richa was already sitting upright, rubbing her eyes. I wondered if she expected to see her bunnies when she opened her eyes.

"Alright." Ravi approved.

"Rimi, do you want to pee now, or later? I won't want you to pee near the wreck. Better slip out and do it now. Here, come here with me." I led her to a spot.

"Now do it here."

"You need to turn the other way mister."

"As if I can see anything." I faced the other way.

I heard a sudden rush of pee and rustling on some dried leaves perhaps.

"Wow, you were holding a lot of it in." I remarked. I felt I needed to pee too.

"Alright, I will take my turn. You face the other way."

"I already am."

Rimi and I headed for the car, passing Richa and Ravi on our way. The SUV was in a worse shape than what it had seemed from the distance. All the windows were broken. Flies were buzzing to glory. I waved my hands to keep them off me. Rimi was doing the same.

"They are attracted by your hair oil." I teased Rimi.

"I don't use hair oil." Rimi sharply replied.

I tried to open the back door. It seemed to be stuck. I went in the side door and pulled the seats down. I picked the bags up one by one and threw them out. I came out and went in the front door and pulled out the radios and maps and my cell phone from the glove box.

"Can I carry my entire bag?" Rimi asked.

"You can. We will take all the bags."

I thought I heard some squeals. I stood their frozen. I moved closer to Rimi. The squeals come from the closest bush. I fished out the flash light from my back pack. I rechecked the pocket to make sure I had the extra batteries there. I thought I should ignore the squeals, should not to disturb the wild life. We carried all the bags and went to our spot.

"Shit, I forgot something." I told the guys.

"What?" Ravi asked.

"My knife." I struggled to think of something.

I headed back. I heard the squeals again. I flashed my light into the bushes. I saw a baby hyena sitting, looking straight at the light. Its yellow eyes shone in the light. It was sitting on its haunches. I wondered why it was deserted. I picked it up.

"What if its mother came back, looking for it?" I thought. But if I left it there, it might even be a kill. I inspected it. It had a gushing wound on its left hind leg. It must have been bitten. Why wasn't it eaten up? That wasn't a question for me to answer any way. I carried it back with me.

The guys were busy fishing in their bags and equipping themselves.

"Is that a baby hyena you are carrying?" Ravi asked.

"Yes. It's hurt. I need to bandage it."

I took out my first aid box, cleaned the wound and bandaged it. It seemed that it was more than a wound. It must have broken a bone. What could I do to help it? I couldn't bear the risk of carrying it with me.

"It has a broken bone. It will take time to heal." I told the folks.

"Can we take it along?" Ravi took it in his lap.

"It would be risky. If the mother hasn't deserted her yet, she might come back looking for it."

"I think the mother has already deserted it."

"Can't say. But, if we leave it here, it might not see the morning tomorrow."

"Let's take it." Richa voiced her approval as she pat the baby's back.

The baby looked back at Richa, as if in response.

"It's so sweet." The mother in Richa spoke. "Let me hold it." She took the baby from Ravi. The moon shone on everybody. We were learning to survive in natural light.

I felt a lot of relief. I could see these friends of mine starting to accept the wild, after the tremulous start. I remembered that it wasn't easy for me too. The sweet memories from my childhood made me happy. The fear of the unknown is the toughest thing to get rid of. I felt glad that these people were learning that the wild is more lovable than we think. Everybody was starting to get aware of the surroundings; the crickets, the cicadas, the owls and a whole lot of sounds that I failed to identify. I lit the backlight in my watch and turned the GPS on. Thankfully, the sky was clear. It would be a few minutes before I got our position. I took my watch off and laid it on the ground. I shone my flashlight and selected a map. I sprawled it open on the ground. I had marked a lot of spots on it, in circles.

"Where are we heading?" Ravi took a position to my side.

"Right at this spot." I pointed out to a spot I had marked with pencil earlier.

"Where are we now?"

"Somewhere around here." I tapped around a spot. "Let the GPS come alive, we would know the exact position."

"That's a GPS?"

"Yup, and very handy."

"Have you ever been in a similar fix earlier?"

"Yes. Not in a jungle though. I have been lost often, in the mountains."

Ravi seemed to trust me more then.

I shone the light on my watch. The GPS was alive. It showed our bearing in degrees.

"There you go. We need to head north east now."

"Were we not planning to stay up a watch tower tonight?"

"There is one close by. It's about a mile, about two kilometers from here. We still need to head north east. The river is in that direction."

The baby hyena had stopped squealing and found a comfortable place in Richa's arms. I folded the map, keeping the origin and destination facing the folds and kept it in my back pocket.

"Richa, do you want to keep holding that baby?"

"I think so." She replied.

"Do you think it's a good idea walking in the night?" Ravi asked.

"No." I answered.

"So why don't we wait here until the morning?"

"Let me think." I did not know what to do for a moment.

"Isn't there any other place, close by?" Rimi asked.

I shook my head in disagreement, I knew I was lying. I wondered why I was doing it; my selfish motives. Did I have to do it? I was risking everybody's lives. They had already walked through a deadly trap. I should have come alone.

"We can't stay here. We have to walk up." I announced.

I thought I wanted to take a few pictures of the wreck, but I let it go. It would have maddened the rest.

"Let's move now." I pulled my backpack on my shoulders and picked up Richa's suitcase. The others picked their bags up and followed. I left the GPS connected and kept checking my bearing. Heading close to the river could have been risky, but that was the best option we had. In about half an hour we reached the watch tower. I remembered it from my last visit. We climbed the stairs.

"Welcome guys. Welcome home. You can now sleep peacefully."

Everybody threw their things down.

"Is everybody alright?" I asked.

"Tired." Richa was the first to acknowledge. "And I feel like throwing up."

She ran to the fence and tried puking. After some efforts she came back.

"I am sure, I feel dizzy and sick."

"Yup, after all this. Here I have something to eat. You need something in your stomach to puke." I took the crackers and jam out while Richa was consoled by Rimi.

Everybody helped themselves. Even the baby hyena seemed to like the taste of jam.

"How about keeping that as a pet?" I suggested.

"Can we?"

"Unfortunately, the government doesn't allow us to." I corrected myself. "Have a good time with it, while we are here. By the way is it a he or a she?"

"We need not know that." Rini said.

I picked the baby up high in the air and checked it.

"A she." I said and looked around. Nobody was interested.

In a few moments everybody was asleep. I erected my tripod along the fence and hoisted my camera. Rimi came and sat next to me.

"What are you doing?" She asked.

"Waiting for the wild."

We heard the first sounds of a pack of wild elephants.

"Those are tuskers. They visit the river every night. All other animals stay low around then."

"Can we see them from here?"

"Unfortunately, no; unless they walk past this spot, while they return. It's highly likely that they do so. The bamboo fields are close by. I hope they plan to visit it."

"Why would they do that?"

"They have fun in bamboo fields. They brush against them. It takes a lot of itch off their back. But it really depends. I don't know. And as long as I can hear them, I can hardly expect to see any other animal."

"Have you been doing all this for a while?"

"I have been to a lot of forests. I love the wild."

She looked down from the tower, through the horizontal bars in the fence. She laid her head on my shoulders.

"Why did those hyenas not attack us, when the three of them were so close to us?"

"When they were fighting for that piece of flesh?" I asked.

I felt her nod on my shoulders.

"Animals don't attack humans. The food chain puts man on top. The animals are very disciplined. They don't break the law of evolution, unless it's an accident."

"Isn't our presence here very much an accident?"

"It is for us, but not for the animals. Their instinct helps them distinguish a prey. We don't fall on that list. If however they do attack us, it's a sheer defense mechanism. It can also be another reason, an imbalance in the ecology. Like when we clear forests, the animals lose their space. Some of the intelligent species have reason enough to attack human settlements, like the elephants. A large cat prefers to stay away from humans, unless sheer chance brings a human close to an injured and famished one. Even then they don't attack for hunger. It's again defense. Later when they smell blood and resemblance to something they can eat, they take to eating. These animals have an immense respect for space."

The elephants never came close to the tower. We heard them arrive and leave. The ritual went on for over two hours. It was bliss for me.

"Aren't you sleepy yet?" I asked Rimi

"I am, but I don't want to miss this beautiful night."

There was silence again. I felt the cool breeze on my entire body and a warm breath on my shoulders. It gave me a strange pleasure.

"Do you have a girl friend?" Rimi asked.

"I have had many."

"Now?"

"No."

She snuggled closer to me. My 'no' for an answer seemed to have made her happy.

"Do you want to know why we are here?" I asked her.

She nodded her head.

"Before I do, I will have to tell you about a gentleman first."

"What gentleman?"

"I came across this man when I was a kid. He wasn't old, but he looked old. I used to go to school at Dehradun. It was a very pleasant walk from my home to school. As much as I loved the walk, I hated my school. The school was hardly fifteen minutes walk from my place, but I used to take a longer route, through the market, passing people, and coffee house. There was also a girl I saw once at a first floor window, during a walk. The desire to see her again, was another reason why I always walked that way."

"Did you see her then?"

"Yes."

"So you did. She must have been your first girl friend then."

"Well I would have loved to believe so, then. But you will be amused to hear this."

"What?"

"She always used to peek out of her window and I used to wave at her."

"And is that all you did?"

"Yes. She was the daughter of a colonel, known to be ruthless, or that's how I knew them from books."

"You never saw her? How old were you then?"

"Around ten. But that is not important. The gentleman however is."

8

Arthur and the Penguins

'The corners are brightly lit,
The saddles are ever moving.
He who stops to watch the angels,
Takes with him a night full of tale.'

A row of hawkers of sweet meat, candies and other knick knacks drew a huge crowd every evening, at a corner in Dehradun. The market was flooded with Chinese goods, but still there were a few practices that would never be challenged; a hoard of people selling knick-knacks and an even larger crowd, purchasing. Everybody has to survive. Everybody has a family to feed, children to bring up, wives to appease and luxuries to settle for. Everyday it's a desire to earn an extra rupee. How well could one sleep over it? The cycle is impenetrable. Ali however, is different. He sits on the pavement, next to the puffed rice man, with his army of clay penguins. Some are as big as the largest rodent, some as small as the imprint on a notebook. He colours them in white, black and blue. Some have fancy orange beaks, some red. Genetic, did you say? Yes, all genes run down from Ali's creation. He has happy penguins, sad penguins, penguin running, and penguin sleeping. People see them, like them. Some purchase, some bargain, some memorize the looks. It's the penguins who rule every day. That day however was different. A kid no more than ten, had been staring at those penguins for a while. He seemed to be getting closer and closer. Ali noticed him, and let him enjoy the moments.

If personal appearance were to be considered Ali would be described as shabby and unkempt. His long white hair dropped all the way to his shoulders, concealing some of the knots that must have entangled over the years. His moustache descended in a smooth milky white fluff and joined his beard to descend to his bosom. He had an old worn out over coat with large plastic buttons, which might have been sewn on later. It seemed as if the coat had been a rich dark blue in its good days, some streaks of the original shade were still visible. His lower half was draped in woollen pants, threads threatening to tear themselves off. His boots were old oxford kind, the layers chipped off from a lot of places; the thread work however was prominent.

The young boy got close enough to actually touch the largest of the penguins. He caressed the wings, up in a happy flutter, and so was the boy.

"Do you like it?" Ali asked in broken Hindi.

The kid was mesmerized more with the bird than Ali. He chose not to reply. He touched it again and nodded in affirmation.

It was bright daylight, close to the evening. There were no customers around; the puffed rice monger hadn't set up his kiosk yet. Ali could talk for some time with anybody who was around.

"Do you know what it is?" Ali asked, to gauge the kind of audience he was addressing.

"Penguin." The boy was in deep thoughts.

"Why, see you already know. Do you know where they are found?"

The boy shook his head. It seems that the school did not teach much, or even if they did there was no personal touch in invigorating a child's curiosity.

Ali was squatting on the floor and the boy in his shorts and shirt, was standing right next to the penguin. He raised his chin to have a closer look at the boy's face. "What is your name?"

"Dev Kumar."

"Dev, what a fine name." Ali exclaimed. He fished for something in his bag and came out with a lump of hair. He put it on the big penguin's head. "See Dev, this penguin now has hair."

Dev had an instant smile on his face. "Penguins don't grow hair on their heads." He replied innocently. His cheeks dazzled with the dimples while he was grinning.

"They sure can, why not?" Ali continued. "Here, come here."

Dev went closer to Ali with a greater confidence.

"Let's see." Ali put his right palm on the boys head. "You are as tall as the penguin is."

Dev looked at the penguin to make sure that Ali was right.

"May be, even as old as the penguin is."

Dev was in consternation.

"Then why can he not have hair while you can?"

That sure threw Dev out of the window. Having come so far in resemblance and agreement, he couldn't back out. He concurred for the fun of it.

"You are joking, right?"

"No, I am not. Even if I am, let's believe that he can have hair." Ali took some burden off Dev's shoulders.

"What else is he missing?" Ali posed the question.

"He needs some garments." Dev had the answer ready.

"Well, sure he does." Ali smiled in agreement. "Don't you have school today?"

"Yes I had, but I ran off."

"Ran off, why?"

"My teacher punished me and made me stand outside. I took the opportunity, jumped the fence and escaped."

"Won't your parents be angry?"

"I will let them be, in any case that's all they do."

Ali had a serious concern on his face.

"How long can you stay here?" Ali asked.

"Well, my school gets over in the evening, so I can just play around until then." Dev had the grin back on his face.

"Have you ever played with clay?"

"Yes, I have these modelling periods in school. In fact I love clay. But I can't make anything like you do." Dev confessed frankly.

"Do you want to learn?"

"Will you teach me how to make penguins? Then I can make penguins for myself and my friends and then we can play."

"Well I can teach you if you want to learn."

"Yes, please, I want to." Dev ran to a small heap of soft clay sitting on a plastic sheet. "Can I make something with this?"

"Here, let me help you" Ali replied and dug a handful from the heap and gave it to Dev. "Now try making a penguin."

Dev immediately sat on the footpath and started working on it, unconcerned that his pants were getting dirty and he might even have to face his mother's wrath. "Won't you make something?"

"Yes, I will". Ali replied, as he watched the boy's enthusiasm and how he was lost in his clay.

Ali kept gazing at Dev and remembered his own childhood, the passion he always had for clay. He took out a bunch of long bamboo splinters and a soft mix of clay. Next he planted all the splinters on the putty and let it stand a foot high. He dug out a big chunk of the clay from the heap and put it on the splinters in a ball. His quick fingers started working on it. He had one eye on Dev and the other on the clay.

Dev came running to him with a finished piece of his work on clay. "Look, a penguin."

"This looks like a sick penguin" Ali responded. He picked some of his tools and reworked it. "How does it look now?"

"Wow, it looks like a happy penguin now." Dev looked at Ali's tools. "Can you teach me how to use them?"

"Alright, I will. Come sit here." Ali made Dev sit comfortably, next to him. "Watch me use these tools." He started working again on the ball of clay on the bamboo splinters.

"What is that?"

"You will have to tell when I am done."

For the next two hours Ali worked and Dev watched. When the work was ready, it was the face of a boy.

"That's me." Dev exclaimed.

"Yes that's you. Do you want to take it home?"

"Can I?"

"Yes you can, but you have to be careful. Take it home and let it dry for two days."

"Yes I will" Dev picked the clay model with the bamboo sticks at its end. "Will you be here tomorrow?"

"Yes I will be, but don't run away from school again."

"No, I promise I won't."

The next day Dev came back in the morning itself. He waited for Ali for a few hours before he appeared.

"What are you doing here?" Ali asked with a mark of surprise on his face

"I was waiting for you."

"Did you miss school again?"

"I have a holiday."

Ali read the bland lie on Dev's face, he was in his uniform. Ali wasn't happy about it. Dev however stared at him helplessly.

Three days went by and Dev hadn't gone to school. His entire day was spent with Ali. On the fourth day Ali saw Dev's arm in the clasp of an elderly man. Dev sobbed, while he was being dragged.

"Is he the guy?" The angry man asked Dev.

A wailing Dev responded with a little nod his head.

The man started swearing at Ali, with all the foul language he could use. Ali listened to him, guessing that he must be Dev's father. He was expecting something like this to happen soon. But Ali had found a good student. He couldn't send him away.

"You, you must move out of here immediately, else I will inform the police." The man cried in rage.

Ali rose and without saying a word started packing. His lean figure stood high, while he started keeping every tool back, neatly in his bag. Dev's father watched him pack everything. As Ali put the last box in, it fell from his hand and hit the ground, scattering all the contents. A large crystalline bead rolled off and stopped at the angry man's feet.

"Where did you get this from?" The angry man asked.

Ali saw the crystal between the man's fingers and smiled. He did not respond.

"Hey answer me, where did you find this from?"

"You would laugh if I answer you." Ali answered in broken hindi.

"No, do answer me. I insist."

"I found it in a mine, in South Africa." Ali's broken hindi evidently proved that he didn't speak the language.

The man moved closer to Ali and examined his face closely. "Who are you?"

Ali smiled. "I am a wanderer."

The suspicion on the man's face grew. "You must tell me who you are." The angry man insisted as he clasped the crystal tight in his fist.

"I travel to learn, I wander to stay, I live to dream come when it may, as you or your son, is my joy indeed." Ali answered in British English .

Ali gathered all the things and put them back in the box. Dev's father put the crystal back in the box and closed the lid shut. He saw the imprint in the box, 'Arthur Mc Cooney'.

Dev and his father saw Ali leave, slowly on his weak legs. The man selling puffed rice came in from the other side, and put his kiosk up.

"Young boy, is that your father?" The peddler looked at the father. "Do you want some puffed rice?"

The father and son only saw Arthur disappear far away.

"What happened to Arther?"

"I kept thinking about him, but one day I found him. I was

going to college then."

"How old were you then?"

"Around twenty one."

"Eleven years later. How did you find out?"

"I met a gentleman at the coffee house. Incidentally I told him about the incident. He immediately told me that he thought he knew the guy. He had come over all the way from England and Arthur was supposedly his grand father."

"So Arthur was British."

"Yup."

"Alright, now that you know you must ask me where we are going."

"Is Arthur and our destination connected?"

"Very much."

"What about it?"

"Arthur stays in a cottage somewhere in this forest." Rimi stared at me with her eyes wide open.

"What?"

"Yup."

"So Ravi was right. You always knew that we were coming here." Her tone was a little disturbed.

I did not answer first.

"If I had told you guys, you would have thought that the quest is a crazy idea."

"I still do think it is. You risked all our lives."

"And took you out of it."

"But you did take a risk."

"But you had fun. You experienced things which very few humans can."

"So this is how you live, endangering your life at every step."

"Not endangering, embracing nature at every step."

"That is your definition, not mine."

There was silence for a while. Her head wasn't resting on my shoulders any longer.

"Do you know where the cottage is?"

"I think I do know where he might be."

"And you are not sure about it?"

I did not say any thing.

"And you surely know the way back."

I shook my head.

"Why are you doing this? You should be going there alone. Get the rest of us back to a safe place." She resounded in anger. "You are an impossible man."

"It's a chance for you to experience the bliss that I do, in the forest, amongst the wild…"

"To hell with your fantasy." She cut me short.

She got up and went where Ravi and Richa were sleeping. She tripped partly in darkness and partly because anger blinded her. I sat there, a little disturbed, but got back in a few minutes. I decided to get rid of the rest, next morning.

9

The green morning

Woken up by a noise I was the first to open my eyes in the morning. The sun wasn't yet up, but I could certainly hear an engine purr. If the wreck was discovered, the watch tower would certainly be checked out. In about half an hour I saw a jeep stop at the base. Ravi and Rimi too were awake. They came running to where I was. I waved my hands at the tourists in the jeep.

"Are you alright?" One of the guys asked me in a British accent.

"Very much. Thanks for coming over."

"We saw the wreck down there."

There were three of them. One of them was a ranger.

All the three came up.

"That was a bad wreck mates." That guy spoke again. "This is David."

"Dev."

"Richard." The other introduced himself as we shook hands.

"D.S. Sharma." The ranger said.

Rimi, Dev and Richa shook hands too.

"You guys must have gone through hell. Is someone still missing?" Richard inquired in a sympathetic voice.

"Nope. All of us are here. It was an accident. The car skid and hit the rocks."

"Thank the great Lord. Seems it took a good beating. It has made a good dining ground too."

"Ya, a leopard."

"Are the ladies doing alright?"

"Richa was a little sick." I looked towards Richa. "Are you feeling better now?"

"And what is that? A young hyena? Where did you find it?" Richard asked.

"It was hurt. The hyenas took to the leopards kill and abandoned this baby. It has a broken bone."

"Here let me see." The ranger offered as he picked up the baby, all alert by then. It stuck close to Richa.

"You must take the permission of Richa though. She is the one who nursed it."

"Good that you brought it along, or else it would have been dead by now."

"Mr. Sharma, can I talk to you for a moment?"

"Yes, sure."

We walked a little away, leaving the others talking to each other. I noticed Rimi listening to us, from the far end. She still looked angry.

"Is Mr. Gulati home?" I asked Mr. Sharma.

"Yes, he is home. Do you know him?"

"I have a favour to ask you." I nod my head.

"Why yes, tell me."

"Can you take these friends of mine back with you and inform Mr. Gulati about the wreck."

"I thought you would come along too."

"No I won't."

"But you can't wander around alone here."

"I apologize for asking you this, but how long have you been around here?"

"A year." He was skeptical while he answered me.

"I have been wandering around here since I was a kid. I know my way."

"But still, I can't let you move around by yourself. Where are you putting up?"

"Chitua."

"Were you coming from there?"

"No we were on our way there."

"How did you take the wrong turn then? The way is well marked."

"Can I have your radio? I want to talk to Mr. Gulati now."

I saw a look of hatred in Sharma's eyes.

"*R 31. Post 112 Green. Over*" *He connected the radio.*

"*R 22. Positive.*" *The reply came from the other side.*

"*Can you have Mr. Gulati on line? Over.*"

A moments silence followed by a buzz again. Everybody else was watching us talk.

"*Gulati here. What is it Sharma. Over.*"

"*We have an issue here. A car wreck at Post 112. All passengers are safe. The leader Dev wants to talk to you. Over.*"

Sharma handed the radio to me.

"*Mr. Gulati, This is Dev Kumar.*"

"*Hey Dev. Good to hear from you. What is all the wreck about? Are you alright?*"

"*Absolutely. I have these friends with me here, in fact four. I added an injured baby hyena last night. I would want Mr. Sharma to give them a ride back. However I have to carry on.*"

"*You just survived a wreck.*"

"*Ya I am alright.*"

"*Dev, I know you know your way around here. But do you want to take a break?*"

"*Not really.*"

"*Alright, carry on. I will get the wreck cleared. However, we would need a statement.*"

"*You know how to work that out.*"

"*Alright. Listen, do you remember Brian Homer?*"

"*Oh yes I do. What about him?*"

"*He was asking about you. I guess he needs a hand.*"

"*Is he on his drive again?*"

"*Yes, cleaning up the jungle.*"

"*Alright, I will be back tonight. I will talk to you then.*"

"*Won't you need a jeep?*"

"*No. I will hike.*"

"*OK. Take care.*"

"Apologies Mr. Sharma, but you have already heard everything." I handed the radio back to Mr. Sharma.

He glanced at me with blood shot eyes.

"I am sure we will be on the same page after a drink." I pat him on his shoulders. "David, Richard, where are you guys putting up?"

"We are at the cottages at Chitua." Richard replied while he looked at David to concur.

"Where are you heading? If I may ask?" David asked.

"Looking for something." I replied.

"What is that, if I may ask?"

"Apologies; can't reveal. However, I can tell you that it's a part of some research I am doing." I lied. I looked at Rimi. She was the only one who knew. Though I knew that Mr. Gulati also knew Arthur but he did not know where he lived.

"Won't you want to go back and pick up a jeep?" David offered.

"Nah, I am alright by myself."

"Alright, if you insist."

"Guys, I am sorry for landing you into this." I turned to Ravi, Rimi and Richa. "These gentlemen can give you ride back. I think you have seen a lot of this jungle for one trip. You need to go back and relax. I will join you after some time."

"Ah, finally; I can go back and sleep for real." Richa remarked. "I also need some tablets. I am still feeling sick."

"You will be alright." I hugged Richa. Everybody started climbing down the stairs. Ravi had got his back pack and Richa's case. Rimi picked up her stuff. I left mine there.

"Hey, be careful." Ravi held my arms.

"I will be." I put my hands on his.

I did not dare to look into Rimi's eyes. When we reached at the bottom of the stairs, I noticed Rimi standing next to me.

"I want to stay with you." Rimi said in a strong voice.

I looked at her in a surprise. I looked into her eyes. I looked down. I couldn't bear staring at her.

"I am staying back with him." She announced next.

"Sister, why are you not coming along?" Richa sounded concerned.

"I will be with you in a while. I am enjoying the forest."

"Madam, you can't stay here. Mr. Gulati made an exception only for Mr. Dev." Mr. Sharma poked his nose in.

"I am staying here. You can come along too if you want to."

"Stupid idiots." Sharma muttered under his breath. "Go to hell."

Rimi and I saw all of them off. The baby hyena showed its preference by sitting on Richa's lap.

10

The Search Begins

I looked around and breathed deeply, taking in the full morning air. The sun was up. The chirping birds that flew around, were everything to me. I liked being with them.

"Who is Mr. Gulati?" Rimi asked.

"The Forest Officer here."

"Don't you want to freshen up?"

"I feel the pressure now."

"Ah ha. There you go. You are about to do something for the first time in your life. It will be fun. Let me be back." I ran up the tower and brought a tissue roll back and a plastic bag.

"Here, hang on to the roll." I handed it over to Rimi.

"Are we going to do something crazy?"

"No, something very natural. Give me your back pack."

She gave it to me.

"Follow me." I led her a few yards away. I dug a small hole with a stick. "Use this hole. Cover it up with mud and weeds around, when you are done."

"Crazy. I should have gone back with them. Stupid me."

"If you can hang on to the pressure until the evening..."

"Shut up. And go away from here."

"I will be up there."

"No, please don't go. Can't you stand over there till I am done?"

I smiled as I walked to that spot and sat on my haunches, locking my knees in my arms.

My meditation was broken by a person's touch. Rimi was sitting next to me, exactly as I was. The sun shone straight on our face.

"Do you feel the joy?"

"I am starting to."

"Do you know that we are very privileged to be spending time here, with nature?" I kept saying as I gazed at the skies, below the sun. The top fringes of the trees outlined the stretch. "Just close your eyes and find yourself lost here." I closed my eyes again.

"Dev." Rimi whispered in my ears.

"What?" I opened my eyes whispering back.

"A squirrel a nibbling at my clothes."

"Don't move." I turned slowly to watch the squirrel.

The squirrel was on its hind legs, standing upright.

"It likes you. It finds a friend in you."

"Does it? Should I touch it?"

"No, don't yet. Something in you has already touched it that is why it isn't scared of you."

"Do you know that tigers in this forest sit next to Arthur, like that little squirrel?"

I looked at Rimi's face.

"Does that not scare you?" I asked.

"A little. But, not a lot."

"I see you have really started enjoying yourself."

"The more time you spend with them, the more you understand them. They get close to you. Humans need a verbal language to communicate, these animals don't. We waste so much of time talking. We miss so much that is around us. They can sense everything. They can sense a friend." I looked at her again. "Welcome to life, as it was."

"I know you prefer staying away from cities."

"Not cities, rather places which have a synthetic layer over them. I feel suffocated, isolated from nature where animals are bred like commodities. Television and electronic games is the favorite pasttime. The rate, at which humans are drifting away behind the guise of evolution, is mortifying. There are so many children who end up growing confused. All they get in the name of education is crafted history. They are taught ways in which to earn a living. Each school, college, institution is like a training house, churning out millions into the work force. Do we ever stop and think? Are we actually the humans the society labels us as? Is a CEO's identity indeed a CEO or for that matter a simple shop keeper? I guess the pace and material wants is too fast for a man to stop and watch." I looked at Rimi. "Why am I telling you all this?"

There was a moment of silence. Perhaps Rimi was thinking.

"I find more comfort here."

"But even in cities we have parks, trees, and even pets."

"Yes, pets. Did you ever have a dog?"

"No."

"I find it sad that so many people leash their dogs around in houses. They keep dogs because it is trendy. How many people actually communicate with their pets? There is so much of blindness that people can't even comprehend that there is a scope of communication. They think that animals are mute creatures who survive on their basic instincts; hunger, excretion, sex and sleep. But that is so untrue. It's a different story for a kid though. Have you ever observed that a kid who has never had a dog as a pet, is scared of dogs in general. One fine day he goes to his friend's place and sees a pet dog. Initially he is scared, but after a few visits, he gets friendly. The kid does it, because his outlook is so natural, in spite of being part of a mechanized society. But for an adult, it's very difficult. He has an impenetrable layer, until one day something opens his eyes. But for most, it's too late. There is so much of sickness, physical problems at an early an age. Why? People live a major part of their lives under the shadow an ailment. Diabetes, heart problems, arthritis, to name a jew, have become such universal grievances. Are we actually addressing the root of all the problems? People now work from morning till night. They hardly find any time for themselves. There is so much of alienation. Vivekananda once said, 'play a lot of football'. Does anybody understand what he meant by that?"

Rimi was lost in what I was saying.

"Let's not talk about all that, any more. Let's live here for the moment." I pacified her.

"I am trying to understand what you are saying. You are so right."

"It's like this. A lot of times we read books which remind us of these facts, but the very next moment, we are back, doing the same things. I would really take the liberty of asking you, not to forget questioning yourself. I don't seek any interest in this. I say this out of love for another human. I really want every body around, every living creature to live a healthy life, live in synergy."

"Hmm..."

"I can't say anything beyond this. I would fail to explain. Let's go up and have something to eat." I gave a big smile.

The grass lands swayed in the breeze. I spotted a few deers spread around.

"Amazing; look at them." Rimi looked so glad.

"Isn't it beautiful? If we go and sit closer, don't be surprised if a deer slowly wanders close to you."

"Won't they be scared?"

"They would be, initially. However, when it realizes that you are not a foe, it will continue doing what it's doing. If you keep up this closeness, you can feed them from with your own hands. They need some time. There have been people who can communicate with animals so well. When we spend more time with animals, we understand their gestures. We should not encroach upon their space. It takes a lot of time before they let you into their circle."

"How long?"

"Let me give you an example. If a Japanese gentleman comes over and wishes to stay with your family, can you accept him right from the first day?"

"No."

"How long will it take to accept him?"

Rimi was silent.

"Think on the lines. He doesn't know your family values, he isn't even aware of Hindu values, though he might be well read." I continued.

"Well, once both of us start feeling comfortable there might be a rapport."

"Exactly, and that happens when he starts understanding the

daily chores at your place. For instance, your mother might feel uncomfortable if he watches her do her daily worship, initially. But when he starts understanding them, she won't. One day, there would be equilibrium; though that involves a significant amount of effort on both ends."

Rimi nodded.

"It is the same with animals, both parties have to put in equal amount of efforts. They are not aware about me and you, about our gestures, about everything we might be doing here. But once we understand them and they understand us, we accept each other. The interesting thing however is that even if we get close to them, for instance this group of deer, it won't mean that we have made it easy for another human alien to them. They would know who we are, but if another person wants to get close, he would have to go through the same slow process. These animals know how to identify very well."

"Amazing. Would it be easier for you though?"

"A little easier; when you get close to yourself, you start seeing and feeling a lot of things. Trust me, the world looks awesome. Let's go up now."

"I saw a documentary on NGEO a few days back. It showed a lioness take care of a baby deer lost in the jungle. The baby was injured; the lioness had her own cubs, and she added it to her litter."

"What happened after that?"

"The baby deer was growing very weak. The lioness was trying her best, but the male in her pride had its eyes on it. Once the baby wandered a little away from the surrogate mother, the young male made a meal out of it. I felt I saw pain and concern in the eyes of the lioness."

"That's an unbelievable story."

"It is. Just consider how many unbelievable things must be going around. Coincidence that NGEO was able to capture this one."

We reached the top of the tower. It looked different from the night earlier. Sunlight was trying to rip its way in through the gaps in the planks of wood, nailed vertically to each other.

"Can't the animals get up on here?"

"They can, but they won't. If however you go out and hurt a baby lion, her mother will chase you to death."

"Ha, ha. And why exactly would I do that?"

"You never know girls. They can do anything. After all they are the superior species."

"Superior species?"

We sat down on the floor as I pulled out the pack of half finished crackers.

"Yes, they are. A female is superior to male."

"The world doesn't think so."

"Funny eh! Just because society claims men are superior to women, men are superior, right?"

"I don't know."

"Consider this. A guinea pig inside a cage, is a human. The scientist and his assistant working on it is the society. The cage has a very small tube as a hurdle. The scientist keeps some cheese at the far end of the tube, but the rat has to pass through the hurdle to get to its meal. After some time, the subject figures its way out. The scientist is happy. He tells his assistant to keep adding to the hurdles. The assistant adds another hurdle to the tube, and keeps the cheese next to it. The rat gets there again. This keeps happening until the hurdles pile up and the rat knows precisely how to get there. Society created some rules and the rat learned. Another rat is added to the cage, it's easier for the second one to learn. The first rat too is a part of the society now. The second rat is a learner, an infant, still learning. What do you think? Is that a real world for them?" I asked.

Rimi looked puzzled suggesting I needed to answer the question myself. The first cracker was ready with jam on it.

"If you consider the cage a reference point, it's the world for the guinea pigs. They might live there forever, if they are not moved for another experiment. But had the guinea pigs not been there, where would they have been?"

"Somewhere, in the wild, perhaps."

"Precisely; somewhere in the wild they would hunt for food. Their first instinct would lead them to the mother's breasts, and then they learn how to feed on other things; the mother slowly passes on her learnings. The mother and others in her species, is the society here. Here they wouldn't have any of those artificial hurdles. If however there is a calamity, they might either perish or learn and adapt and evolve, still, all the hurdles would be very natural. Agreed?"

Rimi nodded.

"What about us? Our school of thought is so contaminated over years of artificiality, material longing, sex, violence, greed, hatred that we can't really call any of our opinions naturally genuine. Even animals have jealousy amongst them; say males fighting for females, but for procreation. They don't have brothels, no courts to back marriages, no judiciary to handle disputes, no blame games. Think about it. Think about a colony of ants and their discipline. What does a male do in any system? It works, for food, for shelter, for sufficing, but who teaches the kids instincts? Who brings up values in the new generation? For an infant a natural choice is the mother. It's a different thing that as a part of this synthetic society a mother has to teach the child how to survive. But she always tries to the best of her efforts to infuse in her infants, what she thinks are values. She is the first teacher. And in this world, no body is above a teacher. Consider the life of any creature. An entire life is a learning process. We are constantly learning. A mother makes the life of an infant easier. A teacher opens the world of awareness. He shows you the way, stops you from wandering. He is making it easier for you. Who is above a teacher then? And a mother is one's first teacher, who is above a mother then?"

Rini was listening very intently.

"Any body you can think of?" I looked straight into Rimi's eyes.

"But fathers also teach their children a lot of values."

"They do, but subsequently. Who does the child pick as a natural choice, while feeding from her breasts? Who teaches the child the first gestures? What would happen to a society where all kids are born in tubes and reared in a hospital?"

"It would be a mechanical society."

"Are you hungry?"

"Yes, extremely."

"Here eat this now. How does it feel like eating, when hungry?"

Rimi ate the cracker. I prepared one for myself and had it.

A few birds landed on the small porch. I crushed a cracker and threw the handful towards them. They took flight, but came back again. Slowly they were hopping all around us as Rimi crushed more crackers and spread them around us. We had a whole lot of crackers with the birds. It was a happy meal. Suddenly all the birds around us flew away. The calm was disturbed by ruffles from the trees. The calm bird sounds sounded disturbing. The monkeys were sending out panic cries.

"There must be a tiger around."

Rimi stuck to me and gripped me hard.

"Don't worry, it won't come up here. Let's get to the porch, but softly."

We dragged ourselves close to the fence.

"Try to keep yourself as invisible as possible." I told Rimi.

We waited for more than an hour, but did not see anything. We saw vultures hovering, a few miles from where we were.

"The tigers usually drag their kills to the outskirts, in the grass lands. Do you know why these towers were erected in the first place?"

"No."

"They have a gruesome history. Historically the British and the rich landlords used to go for games. Some found it easier to erect these posts close to water, where the cats and other animals would usually come over for a drink. And 'bang'. They had a nice and clean shot."

"That's terrible."

"Yes it is. Then with the efforts of some wild life lovers, starting with some passionate dissident British, the games were rationed. Though the Government now has a strict law against the killing of rare species, still, it's tough to get rid of poachers. People think that figures like Maneka Gandhi are useless politicians, finding an agenda for claiming news space, but we need people like them. We need strong voices. We need to spread a lot of awareness. Unless a man starts loving nature, how can he appreciate what is around him?"

"Isn't it tough in a country like India, where people are struggling for basics?"

"I agree. The most basic needs are very tough. Keeping that in mind we have to rear the newer generations accordingly. It's the young ones who hold the keys to the future. I don't say that we should try reform the old. It's a futile head banging. However, let's concentrate on the young." I smiled at her. "And you too are young, so you should concentrate on yourself. Find the teacher in yourself. Every human has that inner voice, but unfortunately we ignore and bury it. We need to teach the children how to listen to it."

I stared at the floor.

"We have such a rich history. The Upanishads, the Gita. All we get to learn from them is abridged extracts in our schools. I won't even call it learning, it's more like memorizing. I will tell you an interesting experience."

I lay flat on the floor and Rimi sat, cross legged, listening to each and every word I was saying.

"I lived in the west for a long time. One stark thing I took objection to was the concept of touching the feet of your elders. I actually started shying away from the act. When ever I used to come to India I tried to escape. I thought the Western concept of calling everybody by his name was better. But now I feel differently. I think that submission and humility is very important for learning for all living creatures; humans are a part of very large system. One can learn from everything that is around us. Only when one is meek and humble, can one learn. It's not just the act of touching one's feet, but the symbol, the humble gesture, that yes I am ready to learn. A small learning can take you far ahead or in other words transmute you ahead in your journey. I think I know why I have these senses, the six senses. To see, feel, hear, smell, and make an opinion. But my opinion is based on such limited information. I see a rose when I am small. I derive some conclusions. I study the same rose again when I am a botanist, I know so much more about it. The second time I used not only the sight, the feel, the smell but I refer books while studying it. I use the books as a source of a whole lot of information, but I can't understand half of it until I talk to the professor. He weaves a nice story from the beginning to the end. What do I do then? I tell myself that I would trust what ever the books and the professor say. I submit myself. I am still not satisfied. I first go to the green house where roses are cultured. But that isn't enough. I go to the natural wild where I can find roses. I want to weave a story of my own. I am trying to go beyond the accessible sources and senses. I am again submitting myself to the rose, its ambience, the nature. I watch what the earthworm does to recycle the earth. I watch the bees carrying nectar. I think and think. Then I conclude that the rose is such an essential part of this biodiversity, the ecology around us and so is each and every flower. I have learnt so much from the flowers, the bees, the earthworm, the insects crawling on the plant, the book, the professor, but it isn't over yet. I will never reach the end of learning, but I can keep walking with that open mind. Would it bother you if I say that among all species, the human being is the only animal that has ego problem? How many times do we really mean touching the feet of our elders when we do it? Different sects, religions do it in different ways. They have their own way of gesturing submission and gratitude. The objective is important and I was cutting that out." I was silent for a moment. "I wonder why I am telling you all this?"

"You can."

I looked over, at the horizon. I wanted to get back to my ambience. The sun was already on top, suggesting noon.

"Hey let me take the steam off. I will tell you an interesting incident. It happened to somebody I know."

"Yes, sure." She looked at me with interest, pulling her top over her belly. I felt she was feeling shy of me. I thought that was a natural recourse.

"I have been to Goa a lot of times. I have a friend, Yuri, whom I met long back. He told me this once, at a coffee table."

11

The Seekers in Goa

"You can take a cab."

"A cab? Isn't there anything more local?"

"Well, for that matter you can try the bus."

"Yup, I too was thinking about some bus. I believe they're crowded though."

"It will crack your ass. Try it."

"Wow. That was a booster. Touché."

The two men were standing on the footpath, next to the bus stop. One of them was a white tourist, the other a brown one. The white man was too white to be an American. Perhaps he hailed from somewhere close to the North Pole. The brown man had a seasoned look. His brows and high cheek bones spoke for him. About forty, he had a serene look in his eyes, mature enough to let the others speak first. The bus stop had a fibre glass top with a brown plastic look, supported by wooden columns. A lady sat there in her Portugese costume, barely noticing the two men. There wasn't a lot of crowd around. On one side one could see the church. The place itself was Church Square in Panjim. A row of motorcycles were parked along the pavement along with a few cars. It must have been free parking. Some of the cars seemed to be waiting for their owners to clean the dust off. What would happen if all the objects around us could speak? May be they do, we are unable to understand with our limited ability. A painting speaks, a caricature does, but how many people understand the language. Would one call it a low level of communication or too niche, intellectually? Who knows, after all its just one's perspective. The white man looked around, a thousand questions haunting him.

"I am Tomas." The white man spoke for himself.

"Hey, I am Yuri." The brown man revealed.

"Yuri, but you look more Indian."

"Ya, I do. My parents named me after that Russian. My father was a scientist."

"I see. I know a lot of people who do that." Tomas said. "That guy would then be Yuri Gagarin, the space traveller." He continued after a brief thought.

"Yes. My father himself would have made that journey. The NASA scrapped him off at the last minute; that was years back though."

"Why is that?"

"Some heart and artery issue".

"Ah, damn. Else you too would have been a celebrity."

"A celebrity? And why would that be?"

"Well, the son of a space traveller…"

"People already call me so, but I have my own profession. I am a photographer."

"What do you shoot?"

"Any thing and everything. Anything that captures my

attention."

"Who do you publish with?"

"I am freelancer. Though I keep selling once in a while to the likes of National Geographic."

"Amazing, then you must be real good at your work."

"Enough for sustenance. Freelancing is a tough profession. Your family always has a reason to grudge."

"Same here man. I feel what ever your profession is; you are always facing a grudge back home."

"What do you do though, if I may ask?"

"I was a French professor. I retired two years back. I taught at a school in London."

"Professor, that's a noble profession. What made you take to travelling?"

"Retired, bored; nothing to do. Wife has her clubs, kids are grown up. You can call it an attempt to release myself from the package that was me."

"Are you successful, yet?"

"I don't know, I am trying to look around."

"What are you looking for?"

"I am looking … I don't really know. I am looking for something though. What makes you think I am looking for something?"

"Let me see. I see those inquisitive eyes and the restlessness. You want to be thrown upon something."

"Ya, something. But what is it?"

"Try my wife, she will leave you panting."

"Hah, your wife. And then you will have a reason to murder me. I want to live a few more years man."

"And what are you going to get out of it?"

"Life, pure life."

"What?"

"Everything. Everything around me. Everything that I have been depriving myself of, all these years."

"And what are those things?"

"I don't know. That is what I am searching."

"What makes you feel you have been depriving yourself?"

"Social norms, superimposing myself on a definitive pattern. Watching the same crowd happy to feed on crumbs and back again to work for it. As a boy I went to a school, was taught things. I was brought up to be good mannered, grow into the society. I was trained to be a part of the social machinery. A big machine that has been running and running. Before I could stop and think, I had my first son." Tomas winked and smiled in askance. "Do you have children?"

"One."

"You know then, what it means." Tomas continued. "Do you want to grab some coffee?"

Yuri checked his watch. "Let's do it. I still have an hour."

"Do you know some place around?"

"Right across the street."

"That place?" Tomas pointed his fingers to a store, which looked more like a kiosk serving tea than coffee.

"Yes. Most of the locals here drink as much coffee here, as tea."

Yuri led the way and Tomas followed. They entered the kiosk. It needed some attention, for instance the corrugated tin shed was visible through the roof. Perhaps they forgot to patch it after some renovation. The walls had some pictures of Goan pastel houses. They needed new frames. The old frames looked worn out. The passage had a row of red plastic chairs and tables. Some of the locals could be seen sitting and so were tourists. Their attires looked colourful. Even the vessels used by the kiosk were painted red on the surface. Tomas wondered if the tea cups would be red too. They found a good spot, just next to the small window, selling cigarettes. Tomas looked at the floor, plastered green. It was indeed rather colourful for him.

"Why do you think they have painted the floor green?"

"I have always seen it, but never found out why. Good question, though. Perhaps it had always been green. I have no idea." Yuri looked down. He then looked at the small boy waiting at a table. He had a brownish cloth on one of his shoulders that he was using to wipe the tables off. The cloth must have been used a lot, it looked faded. The boy's clothes looked a little worn out too. Some of the buttons on his shirt were undone. He was young. He dragged himself to their table in his slippers.

"Can I take the order?" He spoke in English.

"Get us two coffees." Yuri told him. "Tomas, would you take sugar."

"Yes regular sugar please." Tomas instructed the boy. He looked back at Yuri. "I like the syrupy flavor of coffee here. I will stick to it."

They smiled at each other.

"Why don't you teach French at the local university here?"

"No man. I am done. I just want to be a free bird."

"Did your wife not want to give you company?"

"I better not talk about it."

"Alright, I won't ask."

They smiled at each other again.

The coffee arrived. Both picked their cups up and took their first sips.

"Did you explore any of the meditation camps in India?"

"No, I haven't. Actually I have been thinking about them. Give me some leads. I am totally ignorant on that front."

"If you google, you might find all the information. There are a whole lot around here too. Just go ahead and spend some time there. You might find some answers there."

"Are you a part of any of it?"

"Well, not really. I had a go at them long back. I am pretty much happy."

"Lucky guy. Your family must be very lucky to have you around. You must be travelling a lot."

"Yes, I have to. I mostly cover India, especially wild life."

"Wild life; that says it. I met this gentleman on the train last evening. He has come down to India especially for photographing wild life here; has been doing that since the last three months. With the look he had on his face, I guess he would go on for another few months."

"The wild life in South Asia is very rich. Poaching and deforestation, however, has been wiping it off. And did you think that's a shame? Here is more. The NGEO had covered an issue on deforestation in the Amazon basin. It says that while you finish reading a three page length article, forests equivalent to ten football fields are wiped off."

"You take a lot of interest in wild life."

"I do."

"Then let me be bold enough to put it this way. You are the most perfect man I have met to date. You are happily enjoying your work. You seem to have a wonderful family. And you know what, I am more curious now. Would you actually mind if I peek in your life a little bit more? May be you can invite me over for dinner. I beg your pardon, I am taking a liberty. But very frankly speaking, people's lives indeed amaze me. It gives me a chance to weigh myself." Tomas looked at Yuri. "No, you don't really have to do it if you don't want to. I was just taking my chances."

"Sure, I would love to; how about right after this coffee session?"

"Are you sure? I hope I am not being a nuisance."

"Not at all, it's all my pleasure."

Yuri and Tomas smiled at each other.

"You are really being very kind to oblige this sixty five year old man."

"There is a similarity between and you me. I too am a seeker. Please be my guest." Yuri offered joyfully.

"But you had to go somewhere in an hour, right?"

"Yes, I had to go see my family."

"Ah, there you go. Perfect."

Both finished their coffees.

"Let's go. It's hardly a twenty minute walk from here....if you don't mind walking."

"I have my scooter parked there. Do you mind if we pick it up, else I will have to walk back all the way down here?"

"No, sure. Please. We can ride it."

Both walked to the Honda Activa, the most regular scooters on the streets in Goa. Yuri threw himself onto the pillion.

"You need to tell me the directions."

"Go straight and then we will take a left."

"Alright."

They drove through orchids, through driveways saddled

amongst colourful Portuguese houses. They saw young women looking out of their windows. They went past another coffee place. It seemed that they had made a big loop to get back where they started. But that wasn't true, it was just an illusion.

"Stop right here."

They parked. Yuri led Tomas through the gates of a burial ground to two shrines. Some flowers looked freshly laid. A few people were already standing there. Yuri shared a smile with them. Yuri kept a flower on both the shrines. Tomas stood their watching. He still did not know what he was seeking, but he knew where it would end.

"That was moving. Tomas did get an answer then."

"Perhaps he did. Depends on what he learnt out of it. We get answers so often, but fail to inculcate them in our lives."

"I am sure it must have been very moving for him. Even I am moved."

"True, experiences teach us a lot and at the same time we can learn a lot from others experiences. Prepares and tones our minds. We all have an equal amount of learning floating around us; it however depends upon the individual as to how much he can absorb."

"What about Yuri? Did you ever meet him after that?"

"No. We still exchange emails though. He shares with me events that he thinks can be significant for my learning."

"Do you do the same?"

"I write back to him acknowledging how much I learn from him."

"So you are essentially his student."

"Yes I am one of his many students and he is one of my many teachers."

"I too am your student."

"Yes you are, as long as you are learning from me. On the other hand you are my teacher when I am learning from you."

"I don't have anything I can teach."

"You are mistaken. In the entire trip I learnt a lot from you."

"You must be kidding me."

"Not at all."

"Give me one instance then."

"I learnt from you how to stick to someone, even during hard times, in spite of all the hatred in you."

Rimi blushed for a moment.

"Are you blushing?"

"And you are embarrassing me with this question too."

"It's all in the moment Rimi. You find people on the way who are ready to walk with you, until the paths split, though it ends at very much the same spot."

"As for Yuri and Tomas." Rimi shook her head.

"If only we could never forget the lessons, but then we would be perfect."

"How can we do that?"

"Do what?"

"Never forget the lessons."

"Practise revising. Going inside one's self. Picking up the loose ends and laying them straight, in vision."

"How do you do that?"

"Introspection."

Rimi threw a very confused look at me.

"I know it's a tough answer. But that's it. A one word answer." I concluded. "We have had a lot for the moment, I think. Let me take the steam off. Let me tell you about Rupen Banerjee, retired, who wanted to spend time with himself, but a guest tormented him with his presence."

12

The Guest

It was six in the morning. Rupen Babu was taking his morning stroll around the neighborhood. His jaunt went through the small vegetable market leading to an old bridge, hanging over the river. On some days he would stand on it for a while and let the fresh morning breeze blow past him. That would be his best moment in the entire day. He had brought his wife along a couple of times, to share the ecstasy of communicating with the winds. She got over it after a while. Rupen Babu however refused to get fed up of the cool thrill, the breeze brought to his physical self. At a specific moment he would stand along the fence at the bridge facing the east, getting the first glimpse of the sun, below the horizon. What he relished was the fact that there were no buildings to block his vision, because the river ran right across, from north to south. He wondered what had made the river settle for that course. He could figure the outline of fishermen in small boats spreading their nets. The ones that were well off did not need to spread out their nets physically, they had their big nets tied to their hulls. They pulled them out and poured all kinds of fish in large urns and hoisted them back in the waters. The few fish that crossed that course during that split moment were lucky. But that would soon be over when they would be caught in other nets, lurking around. That day, he was waiting for the sun to shine brightly. A large chunk of cloud was not only damping his desires, but also he had to watch it grow dense every moment. In a matter of minutes the daylight grew fainter reducing visibility even further. He had read that deep inside the oceans sunlight couldn't penetrate. Some scientific phenomenon perhaps, he thought he needed to read more. But the river wasn't that deep. He was sure that light reached the depth. But how did life in water react to this sudden change?

Suddenly it started raining. But that didn't make Rupen Babu run for cover, at least not until he felt that he had conversed enough with nature. The rain was another force like the sun. It was as enjoyable.

"Rupen Babu, do you need a lift home?"

He turned back to find Mr. Ghosh in his car. Rupen Babu quick made a calculation in his mind. He did not want to leave. He imagined Mr. Ghosh's croaky voice complain to his wife about the rain and 'the get wet session'. It would be a bad idea to invite his wife's wrath. However, he walked to the car silently and accepted the lift. He kept thinking all along. He was mesmerized by the wonder, called life. A fish couldn't live outside water for long and a human couldn't stand water for too long. And without any of those breathing equipments it would be impossible for a man to stay inside water. As they went through the market he could see fish vendors on the pavement, barely covered with plastic sheets. All Rupen Babu could see, were the dead fish. Again he thought that fish were going off that river faster than they actually should. They were surely not on a vacation. Soon a whole lot of species would be extinct. There must be an ecological system balancing the environment and if these organisms were wiped out, it would mean a terrific imbalance in the aquatic life.

The car stopped in front of his home.

"Ghosh Babu please step in for a cup of tea. It's been a while since we talked last."

Rupen Babu wanted Mr. Ghosh to decline the offer, but he didn't. He hadn't seen a lot of men decline such offers, and that too on a rainy day. Whatever, he did not feel too good about the incidence. Firstly he had to leave against his will; secondly he would have to bear with being a *good host* maybe for the next couple of hours.

Rupen Babu's wife, Kamini Debi, had seen them coming. She opened the door for them and headed back to the kitchen. Rupen Babu could smell warm oil as he entered his house. He asked his guest to seat himself and be comfortable while he changed. As he was going in, he glanced at the chess board which was lying on the corner table. He went close to it pretending to reach the cabinet, stuck to the wall over it, and quickly pulled a cloth, from the couch next to it, hiding it. He then went in and changed and kept thinking how he could get rid of Mr. Ghosh. He saw the framed picture of a village woman standing over a heap of '*rui*'. He pulled the picture out and tore it to pieces. He went to the kitchen to see what his wife was doing. He could smell the spices but unlike other days, it did not reinforce his hunger.

"Go and sit with Ghosh Babu and I will get something for both of you."

"Ok, but what are we getting to eat today?"

"It would be one of your favourites. Now go and talk to him."

Rupen Babu dragged himself to the drawing room. A rush of fear ran through him when he saw his guest smile, mouth wide open. He could see that Ghosh Babu hadn't lost any of his teeth though they were stained red, perhaps with streaks of black. He had never noticed such things earlier. And in front of him was the chess board, ready with the army of ivory pieces in place. The white pawn was sitting at the first move. How he hated the guts of Mr. Ghosh. Rupen Babu wore a smile to compliment the bright idea of his guest. It was in the package of being a good host, not to be offensive to your guest.

"Where did you find this?" Rupen Babu asked pointing at the board, with both his hands.

"It was over the corner." Ghosh babu gestured with his eyes. "It's time now for a good game." He looked at the chess board with heavenly satisfaction.

Rupen Babu knew that it would not be easy to get rid of him, at least not without a game.

"Ghosh Babu what do you think of the Ganges?"

"Why? Ganges is our sacred river. I was planning to take a dip this Saturday. It's been quite a while."

Three pawns from each side were facing each other with the bishops trying to conspire from the safe spots.

"What I mean to ask is have you seen those huge traps for the fish there?"

"Oh yes I have, I think that is a wonderful way to catch fish. Do you know that earlier when they had those small traps with so many individual fishermen, it used to be more expensive than it is now? Now you get *ilish* for the price of a *rui.*"

"Have you ever thought as to what would happen when all those fish are gone?"

"Why would the fishes be gone for sake God's? They are plenty in number. Moreover they keep multiplying."

"Its fish, not fishes."

"Fish, fishes, how does it matter? We are talking about the same thing."

"Do you know how many fish among the ones trapped are still infants?"

Ghosh babu moved the knight to defend his bishop, which was getting to be a direct sacrifice.

"What difference does that make? Fish is fish, adult or kid, all are diet. In fact older fish do not taste that good."

"The fish that are being caught are reducing in number faster, than they are multiplying."

"What makes you think like that?"

Rupen Babu went inside brought a small encyclopedia and opened a page that had been bookmarked.

"Look at this." He pointed his finger to a bar chart.

"This shows the average weight of a single capture 10 years back, which would be in 1970. And this one is a year back. And this shows the rough estimate of the number of traps laid for them. Do you notice the difference? The average weight caught in a single trap has fallen. The number of traps, however, has increased, and so have the consumers."

"That is true. So the number of fishes is falling. But what difference does that make? We will get enough fish for a couple of generations." Ghosh Babu put his index finger across his lips in an effort to flap them.

Kamini Debi entered the room with a tray full of food.

"Ghosh Babu, you should bring your wife too. This is not fair, you men always have a good time, but we women need some time off the kitchen too, for talking."

"Ah yes, I understand. Today it happened so suddenly. I would keep that in mind in future."

Everybody smelled fried fish. Kamini Debi held the tray, waiting for her husband to make space. He quickly dragged another table next to the chess board, for the tray to be placed.

"Have a good game; let me go back to the sweltering heat in the kitchen."

Ghosh Babu swiped his hand close to the fish and grabbed one.

"Wait." Rupen Babu screamed as Ghosh Babu was about to pop a piece into his mouth.

Ghosh Babu was surprised. He put the fish back.

"You can't make that rook move to that square."

Ghosh Babu realized that lost in the aroma, he had made a wrong move. He glanced at the fish with one eye and with the other, at Rupen Babu, waiting for him to pick one up, so that he could follow suit.

He moved the knight back and replayed his turn. The next two moves took almost seven minutes and nobody had touched the fish.

"The fish is getting cold, why don't you take some." Ghosh Babu felt his patience was being tested.

"Do you know Ghosh Babu that the fish consumes most of the algae and organisms, dead and alive, in the rivers? And even those organisms that could be harmful for the humans and animals alike."

"Yes I read that somewhere."

"Did you know that the pollution in the Ganges has been increasing in the last fifty years?"

"Yes I can see that. All that industrial waste accumulates in the rivers and the seas. So many pilgrims wash at the same spot, perhaps forcing a localized pollution."

"This pollution isn't localized; it stretches all the way from the foot of the Himalayas to Bangladesh."

"So how can it be stopped?" Ghosh Babu couldn't resist, and tired of waiting, he picked up a piece of the fish.

"If you stop eating that fish."

Ghosh Babu had again brought the fish close enough to his mouth; his teeth almost ready for the first bite, stopped midway. There was silence for a second as Rupen Babu looked at his face. Ghosh Babu thought there hadn't been a situation where he had felt more stupid. He closed his mouth without taking the bite. He still held it in his hands.

"So you say if I don't eat this piece, this small piece of fish, there won't be anymore pollution, anywhere in the Ganges?"

The heat in the discussion was growing. On one side there was Ghosh Babu, suppressing his urge to consume, driving himself mad, and on the other hand there was Rupen Babu dealing with a guest, that too at a game of chess, against all his interests.

Ghosh Babu put the fish back on the plate. He was controlling his agitation, shaking back and forth.

"Explain that to me."

"Do you know how the ecology in nature works?"

Ghosh Babu wasn't interested in any kind of ecology any longer. The challenge that was keeping him from eating the fish was driving him wild.

The game came to a sudden halt.

"Every time a fish comes out of the water, the amount of unwanted waste in the river increases."

"A single fish is increasing the waste in the river" Ghosh Babu shook his head in madness, eyes wide open and an accent that was more like a challenge than agreement.

"No, the fishing of a single fish is not. But consider the figures when millions of them are fished."

"But why should you be concerned about it? You know as well as I do that if a single person were to stop eating them, it won't stop the millions who eat them daily. You have a noble cause, but how far can that help?"

"I have another reason, and this one is more compelling."

"What reason?"

"It is slow poison."

"What? A fish is slow poison?"

"Not all. But the ones caught in this belt are."

"How can you say that?"

"There are three petroleum processing plants in our vicinity. They have been dumping synthetic waste, which isn't biodegradable, into this same river. Have you even been to 'Kansi ghat'?"

"Why yes I have been there."

The pieces on the board were still moving, but without any thought. Both kept their anger and agitation under control and camouflaged it by continuing to make moves.

"Have you ever touched the water there?"

"Yes."

"Have you noticed that the river water is more pleasant there than the rest of the course?"

"Yes, in fact, I prefer that ghat whenever I have to bathe in Ganges."

"That part of the the river is amongst the most polluted courses."

Ghosh babu raised his eyebrows.

"Haldia plant pours its waste straight into it through an underwater tunnel, at a temperature which is ten degrees higher than the normal temperature of the water. The huge quantity of waste raises the temperature of the river there."

"So that region is heavily polluted."

"Not only heavily, but most of the water that goes inside you, whenever you are bathing, is slow poison."

"That worries me."

"Only think how much of the waste a fish has been consuming. Moreover a fish which is used to living in an ambience of nineteen degrees, would start getting sick if the temperature of the water changes by more than three or four degrees, either way. And the river there is warmer by almost six degrees. This makes those fish sick."

"You mean slow poison."

"Yes I do"

"This thing is serious. Why is nobody doing anything about it?"

Kamini Debi entered the room.

"Ghosh Babu, why, you haven't eaten anything. Come on help yourself."

"I need to get back home. I haven't told my wife where I was going."

"Why? You can use the phone."

"I will come back some other day." He rose and left in a hurry.

Kamini Debi was surprised at his sudden departure.

"He did not even finish the game. That is very unlike him. And he has touched neither the tea nor fish. I don't understand. What happened to him suddenly?"

"He has a bad stomach today."

"And who will eat so much of fried fish?"

"I will." Rupen babu grabbed two pieces of fish and stuffed one in his mouth.

"Ha, ha; that was so mean of Rupen Babu." Rimi said.

"It was, but he did not want to play chess. Mr. Ghosh should have taken the hints."

"Hints can be so misleading sometimes."

"Like when?"

"For instance, you hide the ball and if the doggy sees you hiding it, it thinks you want to play."

"You got me at that. Means instead of hinting, we should be explicit."

"I think so. If we are clear about what we want and what we don't, we can politely refuse."

"Some people are too modest to refuse. But true, too much of modesty brings a lot of torture. A balance is essential."

"Don't we have to look for Arthur? It's late in the afternoon already." Rimi checked her watch.

"Yes we have to. Won't you be afraid of the animals lurking around now?"

"Not as long as you are next to me."

"Let me take a short nap. We will leave after that."

I took a ten minute nap on the wooden floor. I saw Rimi watching down the porch when I opened my eyes. She noticed me waking up and came back.

"Were you bored?" I asked.

"No, I was watching those birds."

I was glad that she was enjoying herself. I wiped my face with my hands. I rubbed the top of my nose with my shirt, to dry the sweat. It was warm. I got up and picked my back pack up. Rimi did the same.

"Let's go."

We came down the flight of stairs and took the closest trail.

"We will walk on this one. Watch out closely for any signs of paw marks. Animals are gentle, but we must be cautious. We will keep our ears and eyes open for any unnatural signal. You will see that it's very easy to live here."

We kept walking.

"It's good we don't have Richa with us. She is better off at that rest house." Rimi remarked.

We stopped when we saw some fresh paw marks.

"Bear." I said.

"Can it be somewhere around?"

"It might even be watching us. But the paw marks run this way."

They were leading diagonally, behind us.

"We are going away from it. It shouldn't bother us. A whole lot of other animals are watching us."

The evening was falling. We saw some smoke rise at a distance.

"Is that some settlement?" Rimi asked.

"It should be, else a forest fire." I tweaked the buttons on my watch. It told me the elevation. "We are a thousand feet above the sea level. We will find out what that smoke is."

I turned a little away from the trail. We walked through the bushes, that reached my hips.

"Watch your step. Step in where ever I do."

I was keeping an eye on any possible scorpions, snakes or any of the creatures in the bushes. After hours of strenuous walk, we reached a spot where we could see a valley. The plush green valley had a thick coat of green.

"My goodness; look at that." Rimi remarked.

We saw fire glimmering like stars. It was a spectacle.

"Miss, you are witnessing a rare fire in the forest."

"Can't we inform somebody and stop it?"

"It's a regular thing; comes and goes by itself. Let's sit over that rock."

As we sat next to each other the fire was slowly spreading. It led to pockets of smoke. Brilliant sparks were dazzling us.

"Do you know what *aurora borealis* is?"

"I think I have heard about it. Is it the brilliantly lit night skies?"

"Precisely; it's the sun lighting the skies up in different colours."

"Have you ever seen it?"

"Yup, I have been fortunate enough to see it once. You need to go further north though. It's a common sight in North Canada, Alaska, Greenland and the likes."

Suddenly I had an idea. I took my camera out.

"Here, you sit here, facing that direction. I will take a few pictures with the fire. You can use them when you are getting married." I teased her.

"You can take the pictures, but I won't use them for any marriage."

"Alright, sit over them and remind yourself of this moment."

I adjusted my portable tripod and fixed my camera on it. I took a lot of pictures. Some with Rimi, some without her. She let me do what I wanted. She was enjoying herself. I went back and sat next to her, packing every thing back.

Rimi kept her head on my shoulders.

"Are you getting ready to fall asleep?" I asked her.

"I wish I could. Can you sing me a lullaby?" She asked innocently.

"My lullaby will invite others too. What if a tiger comes around and asks me to keep singing and then brings its entire family? 'Keep singing else I will eat you up'."

"We can take turns. I will sing when you are tired."

"How long can you sing? What if your own lullaby puts both you and me to sleep?"

"Then we will become a happy meal for the tigers; nothing better than dying here."

I thought for a moment. Peace and happiness makes one so fearless. I felt her cheeks with my rough hands. I put my arms around her and hugged her tightly.

"What will your boyfriend think if he sees us here?"

"I am glad I don't have one."

The warmth in her body was intoxicating. I wondered whether the woman was getting me but then I corrected myself. I thought that I wouldn't analyze or question myself for once, and experience everything as it came.

"It's getting darker now. We must move on."

We resumed our journey. I was fine with my back pack, but Rimi's back pack was too big for her. She wasn't used to trekking for so long. It might tire her soon enough.

"Are you tired?" I asked her.

"A little, but not much."

"You are carrying a lot of load. It would tire you."

"It's ok for a while."

"We can transfer some of your stuff to my bag."

"I can carry my luggage."

"Alright. But let me know if you feel tired." I had some water and passed it to her.

It had gotten pretty dark, but we could smell grilled meat.

"Rimi, we are almost there." I hugged her tight.

"Ahh. You are too strong for me. You hurt me."

"I am sorry. I just transferred some of the joy."

"That wasn't joy. That was pain." She pinched me hard. "Magnify that and that's how I felt.

"Aww." I cried out.

"You mean girl. That was deliberate."

"That was a reaction."

"I will remember it."

"And so will I."

"I am walking away from you."

"And I am following you."

"You can go your way."

"I will sit right here then."

"Sit here and make love with the monkeys."

"I will make love with whoever I want to. You need not tell me."

She sat where she was. I moved on and hid behind the bushes, watching her. In a few moments I could hear her crying.

"I know you are there." She cried.

"No, I am not." I replied after a pause.

I felt silly and stupid. I walked back to her, picked her up and hugged her again. She resisted, then gave in. I felt her wet cheeks with mine. That time I made sure that I did not squeeze her.

"Let's think that the last hug never happened. This is the one that was supposed to be and carry on."

She kept standing there, sniffling and drying herself on my shirt.

"You should make more noise when you weep or cry. How else would others know that you are crying?"

"How else did you think you came to know that I was crying?"

"So you tricked me?"

"Did I have a choice?"

"The womanly tricks, I swear I won't trust you next time."

"We will see."

She held both my cheeks between her palms, pulled my head down and kissed me on my forehead.

"Trust me, we are being watched. And if somebody feels the pangs of jealousy, then you will have it."

"Like who?"

"Like that monkey again."

"Why do you think you are better than a monkey?"

That got me thinking. She closed her eyes and embraced me, clinging to my chest. Her arms went under mine and over my shoulders.

"Where did you learn that?"

"Learnt what?"

"Taming a monkey?"

She opened her eyes and gave me a mischievous smile and found her place back on my chest.

"I think we are forgetting that we are standing in the middle of a jungle."

"You have to worry about that, not me." She firmly replied.

"You have wet my entire shirt."

She just clung to me and did not answer.

As we walked, I felt a sudden pinch on my neck. I looked at Rimi, she had a small dart in her neck. It was covered in red and orange feathers. I raised my hands to her neck and pulled the dart out. Next I pulled mine out. Before I could analyze, I was knocked out.

13

The claustrophobic cell

I woke up and saw walls made out of bamboo, all around me. Rimi was still asleep. Sunlight was pouring in thin beams, through the gaps. I heard voices around, outside the cell.

"Shivao, akera biknu mar te."

"Kere maigo naita." Another voice replied.

It was all a bantering for me. It wasn't any language. I tried waking Rimi up. I shook her harder. Her clothes had dirt all over them. Her cheeks looked muddy. I thought she was looking beautiful. I checked myself, I was equally dirty. My clothes had lost all colour. I saw a bowl of water, made out of skin, near the door. I picked it up and checked out my reflection. I couldn't recognize myself. Rimi opened her eyes.

"Are we dead?" She asked.

"Better than dead."

The shouts from outside increased. I heard the sound of approaching footsteps. It stopped near the door. The door opened. The sudden light forced me to close my eyes. When I opened them slowly, I saw a tribal, in front of me. Naked, with a stick in hands, he stood erect while holding the stick upright. His penis wasn't very large. He knitted his eye brows when he saw me checking his private parts out. I quickly changed the direction of my gaze. Rimi had huddled back. It was sheer surprise for her as well.

"Karche lim nao ture." The tribal said something.

I did the first thing that came to my mind. I lay flat on the ground, on my chest. I folded my hands as in worship. I gestured Rimi to do the same thing. The tribal pounded his stick on the ground. I felt that he was impatiently trying to ask us something.

"Ta ba inkin doa natiake?"

His tone suggested that he was asking a question. This could have an answer only as a yes or no. I looked up towards him and turned my hands in front of my mouth and then my ears, trying to say that I can't understand what you are saying. My dumb charades skills were being put to a severe test.

"Gujukatima"

I felt that he said 'idiot' it was more from his expression than what he said. I tried to sit up, but he pounded his stick again. I kept lying where I was. I closed my fingers in unison and brought them close to my mouth and then turned to my side and rubbed my palms over my stomach and then looked at him.

"Kaounttine, juju mastehichi."

I made an innocent face with all my skills. He waved his arms over his face and turned back and went out. He did not close the door. He walked to some distance and told some one something. I hoped it was for good. I sat up and so did Rimi. I did not see my bag and neither was Rimi's around. My watch was gone, my precious watch.

"Alright, don't be scared. These people mean no harm."

"Who said I am scared? He was completely naked."

"Are you aroused?"

"Shut up."

"I am excited. I want to meet the tribe."

"Are you scared of anything?"

"I don't know. But I am excited."

"We are in a mess. What makes you excited?"

"I will see naked women in a few minutes." I grinned in satisfaction.

Rimi shook her head in disbelief.

"I am worried." Rimi acknowledged.

"Don't be. I told you they are harmless."

"I am worried about Richa. She would be panicking. They would have expected us back."

"That is one useless baggage. That is why I prefer travelling alone."

"You are so mean and selfish."

"What did I do now to deserve that?"

"It's just the way you think."

"Are we ready to fight again?"

"I want to thrash you hard for landing me into this."

"You chose to come along."

"I knew you would say that. You are unbelievable."

I crawled to the door, to get a better view of what was outside. I saw a lot of them sitting around. I quickly crawled back to Rimi.

"The women are naked."

She tried to hit me, but it landed on my back. I had barely escaped it. I crawled back to the door.

Right then the tribal man came back, thumping, as he was

walking. I went back to my position before he could notice and went back on my belly. Rimi kept sitting.

"Tama tama." He gestured with his hands to get up.

I stood up first. Rimi followed.

"Mootan, para para." He gestured to follow him.

He turned and started walking back. I started walking and dragged Rimi along.

"See, I already think that I can understand him." I told Rimi.

Outside, the view was beautiful.

"Don't you think the world, the skies, in short everything looks better when people are naked." I teased Rimi.

"Go and have some babies with them." She replied tartly.

We were led inside a small hut made out of bamboo, among a row of similar huts. I joined my hands and bowed in front of everybody sitting there. I tried with all my gestures to explain our situation. I crossed my fore fingers to and fro to suggest that I was taking a walk and then swayed and fell down to suggest that I was suddenly knocked out. The women sitting there laughed as they saw me do it.

"Itu para titake?" The leader asked me.

I shrugged my shoulders.

"Kittane, karbar inki titake." He ordered one of the men.

I saw the ladies staring at me. One of them was suckling a baby. I did not dare to look at them, lest I gave away my curiosity. Offence was the last thing I wanted to attempt at that moment. The man came back with a sheet of folded paper and gave it to the leader. The leader opened it and gestured me to come closer. He then handed the paper over to me. It was a bond paper. The title read 'Government of India'. I scanned the contents.

A paragraph with some strange symbols led to another in English.

'This person has come to meet the sect 'Kinuka' with the full approval of the Government of India. He is doing research work for the benefit of the tribe. The Government is highly thankful for your hospitality.'

It was signed by the president of India. I pursed my lips and looked at the leader and shook my head. I again flooded as much innocence as I could.

"Titake, kotna ichoos titake." The leader questioned me gesturing, where is it.

I understood one word, 'titake'.

"No Titake." I shook my head.

I noticed that our bags were being inspected at one corner of the room. I felt sad for having disturbed the privacy of these people for a moment. But then, they were the ones who darted us. I receded from the spot and sat on the floor cross legged, resting my head on my open palms. I stared at the ground. I looked back at the leader. He was staring at me. He was elderly. He must have been somebody's father too. I gestured with my hands and stomach that I was hungry. The leader kept his silence. Then he said something to one of the men. The man came to me and gestured me to get up. He too had a stick in his hands. One of the women took Rimi with her. I was led to a stream. The man gestured at me, rubbing his hands over his arms and body and then pointed to the stream. He was asking me to wash myself. I took my clothes off and immersed myself in the cold water. I washed myself all the way, while the man stood there, watching me. I only hoped that he wasn't gay. I wondered whether I should dress up. I thought I would live their way. I decided not to dress back, when I got out. The man looked at my fly. It was certainly bigger than his. He pointed towards my garments and then gestured that I wear them. I discarded my underpants, wore my trousers and carried my shirt along. I dipped it in the stream and wrung it out. I felt fresh. I decided to hold my shoes in my hands too. I wanted to spend my time with my hosts, like them. I was led inside another hut. Everybody turned to look at me. I bowed my head in a mark of greetings. I saw a large flat vessel and two huge roasted boars sitting on it. Around fifty men and women were sitting around. A few babies were wailing. I tried looking for Rimi. She had washed herself too. Her hair was wet. She wasn't in her dirty clothes. She was wearing a khaki colored apron. Somebody must have lent it to her. She was barefoot. I hoped that she wasn't a vegetarian. The leader cut a piece off the pork with the knife sitting next to the pot. Everybody was silent until then.

"Kintua haibee". Every body said and one by one cut a piece for themselves.

When my turn came I picked up the knife and cut a piece. One of the men helped me do that.

"Haibee." He said pointing out to the pork.

"Haibee." I nod my head. I learnt another word.

I like roasted pork, though I preferred beef better. Nevertheless I was sure I would enjoy the flavour. I was worried about Rimi though. She had the piece in her hands and was struggling to eat it. The women were giggling and laughing at her. I seemed to be in sync with the men. I made all the satisfactory gestures about how the food tasted. They all seemed to have taken my word and approved of me. Two men then brought in a large pot with some liquid in it. I could hear it lapping. The men inside were singing. Each man walked to the pot, picked a ladle full up and drank it.

When my turn came, I could certainly smell the hint of liquor. I felt glad. That was something I needed most. I was trying to sing with the men. I was sure that Rimi could adjust herself, when she saw me having fun. I was thrilled about my turn. I danced more out of excitement. I could happily add another flavour to the list of liquors I had tasted in my life.

"Jiga." One of the men told me, pointing out to the drink.

I took a mouthful. It tasted bitter, worse than cheapest vodkas in USA. I had never tried country made liquor in India, so can't compare. But, that was one shot. It threw a thrust in me. In a few moments I started dancing with the men. We walked out of the hut after a drink, each. There was a huge fire outside. We danced and kept dancing. I felt I had known those people for ages. I noticed the women sitting at the far end and watching us. After some time, the men made space for the women. The women danced, while 'we men' watched them. I laughed at jokes I did not understand. I shook hands with them, wrestled playfully with them. I displayed how strong I was, started doing some pushups. The men gathered around me, started counting in their own language. I was done at fifty, by my own counts. They cried together when I fell flat on the ground. One of the men was pushed forward He started doing pushups. I stopped counting after fifty. The men kept counting. It must have at least a hundred, or even a hundred fifty. One of the men then came forward and stood upside down, over his arms. I was challenged. I shook my head, trying to say that I won't be able to do it. Their strong encouragement forced me to attempt make on. I fell hard on my back. One of the men helped me do it. My arms were crying out in pain. I lay on the ground tired. I raised myself back on my feet again. The men came to me one by one and shook hands with me.

They dispersed, and so did the women. I did not see the leader. A man took me to a hut. It had a nice floor made out of bamboo shoots. Rimi was already sitting there, her feet straight. The small oil lamp looked feeble, after watching the big fire through the night.

"Everything happened so fast Rimi." I threw my head on her legs. "I am stoned like a devil."

"These people are nice."

I turned my face up and looked at her. I noticed a necklace stringed in beads around her neck.

"Did you get that here?" I felt the beads. "These are carved out of bones. Amazing."

A woman then came in and told Rimi something. Rimi shook her head. She closed the door behind her as she left.

"What did she say?" I asked Rimi.

"She said, sleep well."

"You understand their language already?"

"A little; these women taught me some words. Like 'neeche' for sleep. And do you know what the name of their leader is?"

I shook my head, I did not know.

"Glian. Do you know what the name means?"

"No." I tried to make sure that I understood what was being said inspite of my dizziness.

"The son of nature." She added.

"Did you have any drink at all?"

"No. The women don't drink. Only the men do."

"I wonder what it would have been like if the women did too. Seen any of those parties at the Goa beaches?"

"No. What do they do?"

"They all drink and dance and keep dancing. You missed a lot of fun."

"I had my own share of fun. What did you guys do?"

I told her everything about the pushups and the games, the 'manly games'.

"What did you do?" I asked her.

"These women showed me their shacks. I played with babies. I met grandmothers. Do you know how they address each other?"

I looked at her in curiosity.

"*Tinna* mean man, *tinni* means a woman. *Popo* is father, *Nu* is mother. The most interesting are the grandparents. Oops I forgot. It's something like *manta* and *manti*. I am sure I am not pronouncing it right."

"I am glad you had fun."

"You too had, right?"

I nodded my head in agreement.

"They think we are a couple."

Rimi nodded her head.

"Should we not do then what a couple is supposed to do?" I teaser her.

"No."

I hugged her belly. She was rubbing some kind of a gel on my face and my body.

"What is that?" I asked.

"Insect repellant. Help me put it on you."

Like a good kid turned all around slowly. She put it all over me. I cuddled like an infant when she was done, my head still in her lap.

"Am I in love with you?" I asked her.

"I don't know."

"I am drunk, though."

She was brushing my hair with her fingers. It worked; I was asleep in no time.

14

A morning too beautiful to be true

When I woke up, I did not find Rimi. The door was closed. I turned my wrist to check my watch, but it wasn't there. I remembered I had been stripped. I rubbed my eyes and stood up. The sun found its way in. I presumed it was late in the morning. I realized I had splitting headache. I opened the door a little. I saw Rimi standing outside among a few women. I could hear the low hum of their conversation.

"Rimi." I called in a low voice.

One of the women pointed out at me. Rimi turned to look. I felt the woman told her to come to me. I thought that had this been a city, the first thing she would have done would be to shout back and ask what was up right from there. But these women had a different upbringing. They spent their lives serving the men. They were taught to be meek. I wished I could stay there forever. She walked to my coyly. I thought she was learning.

"What happened?" she asked when she was close to the door.

"Can you come in?"

She came in. I closed the door.

"What time is it?"

"I don't know."

"How long have you been up?"

"A few hours."

"I have a terrible headache."

"The drink is still working. Have it again tonight."

"Tonight?"

She smiled.

"We should be leaving. We have to find Arthur." I added.

She kept smiling.

"What are you smiling at?"

"Nothing."

"A woman should not be so happy. I smell something fishy." I moved straight in front of her face.

She did not stop smiling.

"You need to brush. You have bad breath."

"Where do I get a brush from?"

"They have something powdery stuff you can use."

"A tooth powder? These people brush?"

"Yes they do and they have the healthiest teeth I have ever seen."

"But why are you acting so weird?"

"Me? Weird? Not at all."

"Tell me one thing. We did not have sex last night."

She shook her head.

"Oh yes, if we had it you wouldn't be happy. I forgot the woman's side. But something is wrong."

I pushed her down on the floor and made her sit next to me.

"I told them we are not married."

"Among everything what the hell made you tell them this?" I made the weirdest face possible.

"The women asked me in the morning."

"I don't understand. What do they have to do with this?"

She shrugged her shoulders.

"So what's the big deal if we are not married? We did not have sex."

"Since we slept together, they want us to get married."

"Married? What crap? We hardly know each other. Its only been two days that we have been together."

"They have a custom. A man and a woman can't sleep together unless they are married, and since we already have, we must get married."

"What nonsense? They have no rights interfering in our business." I said in agitation. I heard the women whisper outside our door. I realized I was being loud.

My response had certainly taken the smile off Rimi's face.

"These people expect us to do it. Tell them you don't want to."

"And then get skinned alive. They have very strong beliefs."

We looked away from each other, facing two different directions in the room. The women were still whispering outside. I could see their shadows through the gaps in the wall.

"Alright, we will fake it." I announced. "Let's not get too personal here. We will do it for an experience. Both you and I will get something to learn out of this. But we are not having any relationship. It's too early. I am not ready yet."

Rimi nodded.

"Why are you crying now? Do you remember why we came over here? We came here to have a trip. How on earth did you start believing in what these people are saying? Are you in a sane frame of mind?"

She started weeping.

"They want us to get married tomorrow. I am not supposed to see you until then." She rose and went out. I heard the women console her. They all went away. The mad lot.

I threw myself on the floor, pulling my hair. I wondered why Rimi was taking it seriously. Worse, I was not going to see her till the next day. She had at least started understanding their language. I was at the far end; living on gesturing. She was certainly more adaptable than I thought she was. I decided to go out and have fun. We could not go back at least for the next few days. I thought I should run away. I laughed at myself. Run away from what? That wasn't serious. The splitting headache was killing me. I decided that I would not drink that night. I wondered why our absence wasn't bothering Rimi any longer. Wasn't she thinking about Richa? Could someone transform, when the ambience was congenial? Rimi always seemed to be the silent one, watching things closely, never making an opinion in advance. What was in her mind? What was she thinking? I had no way of knowing. I wouldn't be seeing her for some time. I was disappointed. Something was getting hold of me, what was it? I hadn't been like this. Things had never bothered me. Did they actually mix some black magic in the drink? Suddenly I felt I wasn't in control. I thought I could converse so well with animals, nature, humans, but that woman, there was something about her. I was sure I could get over it. More than me I was sure Rimi could get over it. It wasn't my own self that was bothering me, but her. She could adapt so well, faster than I did. She was picking up the language faster than I was. Rimi told me the equivalent of sleep, the night earlier, and I had already forgotten. I hadn't been like that. I thought I was a fast learner, but that woman beat me. She was living in the present, while I wanted to move on. But what *was* the present? Was she in love? I felt it too, but so often it's the momentary obsession. How could she be so sure? The tribal marriage wasn't any reason to make me upset, but the look in her eyes. The fact that she was getting so close to me was upsetting. What if I actually did escape? What would happen to Rimi? I could get back to Chitua and send someone to get Rimi back. I knew my way around. Hell, I did not have my watch. It was a handicap. Could I find my way without my compass and GPS? I could take a chance. I felt jealous, jealous of Rimi. She looked so happy. I wasn't, after a long time in my life, I was worried. What if I actually married her, the tribal way? We could go back to Delhi and every thing would get back to normal in a few days. I have had so many women in my life earlier; she would be another one, an unintended one. So would I be for her. I thought I would let what ever was happening. If Rimi was taking this seriously, it was her problem, not mine. I was a free soul, and would always remain free. I got up, having made up my mind. I thought I should go out, freshen up and play around with the kids, or even go out hunting with the men. I pulled myself up and dragged myself out of the room. The sun was blinding me. I squeezed my eyes. I had dust all over me. I felt my cheeks, felt the bristles. I put the other hand on my forehead, providing a shade to my eyes. I saw a few men standing over a log of wood. One of the men was getting ready with his axe to chop it off. I went close and smiled at them. They did not respond. I stood there. Nobody looked at me. I did not understand. The man started chopping hard. I wanted to work off some energy. I wanted to chop the wood myself. Anything to take all thoughts off my mind. My muscles were aching for some physical work. I stopped him and gestured, asking if I could help. He handed the axe to me. It was the heaviest axe I had ever held. I asked the others to move back a little. I held it back over my head and dealt the first blow. I made sure that my grip was tight enough. Years of squash had given me a strong grip. My body, my arms moved in sync with the axe. I felt the heat emanating from me. I felt the sweat, but I kept going. I kept hitting the wood with all my might. I had become a robot for the moment. I had forgotten everything else. I couldn't see the men standing around me. I didn't remember where I was. I was nowhere and everywhere. It was just me, the axe and the wood. In a while my legs were numb. I felt I did not have any kind of physical existence. I wasn't even aware about chopping any longer. I just kept hitting at the same spot. I kept going until I dropped to the ground. Slowly I opened my eyes. The men stood there, bent over me. One of them extended an arm and pulled me up. I felt the ache in my legs. I felt each and every muscle I had put in all they were worth, to help me stand. I stood there, sweat on my chest, my face. I looked at the rest. I thought I looked more like them. They clapped their hands. I looked at the log of wood. The huge log was almost in two pieces. One of them went ahead and finished the job. Another man helped me walk. I threw myself under a tree. I wanted to wash myself. I gestured at the man that I was going to the stream. He understood and let me go. I remembered the directions from the previous day. I took my trousers off and walked straight into the water. I floated in the water for a very long time. I had practised floating since I was small, without moving my arms, just with my breath. Sometimes I used to fall asleep like that. I must have slept, I don't know for how long. I was tired; oblivious of the world. When I opened my eyes the sun was still up. I raised my head to look around. The surroundings did not look familiar. The water must have carried me downstream. I wondered how far I was. That did not bother me however. I wanted to spend time with myself. I started swimming towards the bank, until I felt the pebbles under my feet. I noticed some crocodiles lazing in the sun. I got back into the water to move further downstream. I noticed a group of hippos. A small pocket into the side had collected some water. They hardly noticed me. I tried not looking at them directly. I simply stepped out and lay on my back. I thought I would spend some time around the animals. Crocodiles could sometimes be dicey, though. I took a quick glance at them. They were not moving. I rested again. The hippos started playing again. I got up again and walked deeper into the jungle, keeping in my mind the upstream direction. I had to walk that way. I turned to my left, when I found a trail. I could still hear the stream. It was fine as long as I could hear it. I noticed a lot of new kinds of trees on my way; different birds, I had never seen earlier. I looked up a huge tree. I saw a black thing up there. I stopped and tried looking at it intently. It was a black panther. I stood there. We kept watching each other. It was purring. I backed up and went around the tree. In a few minutes I was back on the trail. I kept walking. It was painful walking barefoot. I tried being careful so as not to step on thorny bushes. In one of my earlier sojourns in a forest a certain plant brushed against my bare legs and had left me covered with a rash and blisters. It took half a month to heal. I certainly knew what that plant looked like, but there could be many more, different kinds. Once in a while small thorns did find their way into my feet. I pulled the ones out that were painful. The ones that did not bother me, I let them stay. I had taken a lot of thorns earlier. I remembered when I used to go the roof of my house, to fly kites. Broken pieces of furniture were sprawled all around. Some had nails in them. I knew where they were piled, but sometimes I used to get so lost flying, that I would suddenly step on a nail. It was painful when it went in, an inch. But the pain used to be momentary. A red circle highlighted the nail, on my foot. I knew I had to pull it out in one jerk. My kite meanwhile would be somebody else's prize. I would pull out the nail. It was never bloody. I guess we have a very thick skin on our feet. But it used to be painful walking for the next few hours. When I got used to the experience, I stopped bothering about a nail and kept flying. Only when I lost my kite, would my attention go back to the nail. Sometimes I used to walk bare feet on the tar streets, just for the experience. The barefoot rickshaw pullers, fruit mongers made me curious. If they could walk without shoes, I could too. Later I used to do it a lot, while coming back from school. I used to keep my shoes in my bag, and walk. Feel the heat on the streets. Slowly I got used to it. All this had given me enough confidence to walk bare foot on the wild trails too. But you never knew. I had to be careful. I saw a dead bird, lying on its back. I went closer and picked it up. It fluttered its wings a little. It wasn't dead yet. I felt a small dart on its back. It had the same red and orange colored feathers. I felt sorry for the bird. I knew the tribals were around. I heard some muffled footsteps. A man in the tribe, who I knew by his face, came and stood next to me. He took the bird from me. He had a very narrow bamboo, about two feet in length, in his hands. He had a thick skinned belt around his waist and a few darts were hanging from it.

"Would you be using this bird for a meal?" I used gestures while I spoke slowly.

He nodded.

"Are you going back or will hunt further?" I asked.

"I would still be hunting." He answered in his own language.

I followed him, wherever he decided to go.

As I matched his steps, I felt more like him, entirely naked, athletic. I felt more energetic. I was in the moments I had been longing to be in. He was walking very softly. I imitated him. He cupped his ears in a direction and looked at me. He pointed out to another tree. I saw a pack of macaws between the branches. He stepped a little closer to get a clear vision. He thrust a fresh dart in at one end of the bamboo gun, the pointed end away from him. He put the other end in his mouth, aimed and blew heavily. The dart found its way straight into a macaw. It squealed in surprise. The others fled. The birds on the others trees also took flight. The monkey tried getting away, but in the next couple of seconds fell through the branches. He got stuck in the lowest branch. My mate climbed up the tree with quick movements and shook the monkey to the ground. He got back to the ground and found a thick piece of short wood. He took out some slices of bamboo and tied the front paws of the macaw to the center of the wood stick. He handed me the log with the macaw tied. He turned around and held the stick behind his neck, with both his hands around the edges. The monkey was hanging behind him. He started walking. The bird we just killed hung next to the darts. The monkey was facing me, while we walked. Its body and tail dangled in motion, with my mate's gait. The monkey was huge and heavy. The man swayed while he walked. He had to put his foot straight on the ground while he shifted his weight. I felt like walking behind the pied piper. The only rat alive was me. I thought I would get used to it. Killing an animal wasn't fun, more for me who promoted animal conservation. But that was a tribe, who survived on primitive means. I thought of the moments when I feasted on different kinds of flesh. I liked the flavours most of the time, but always tried to forget that they were kills. I had screened myself from that fact. Recently I came to know that China bred tigers for soup and flesh under the guise of conservation. At least the tigers were alive, for whatever excuse, but ecology and natural bio-diversity was fading below the horizon. Small pockets of tribes are essential. They introduce us as much to the meaning of life as we try to introduce them to modernization. The hard core tribes however refuse to embrace all this. We need the Jews who isolate themselves from the worldly modernization and machinery, orthodox for example. Not only were they staying away from the synthetic lifestyle, but also keeping the vices that paralyze our thoughts, at bay. So are these tribes. They don't need a lot to be happy. Each and every work around them required human labour, enough to keep them occupied for the day. The nights are sometimes spent regally, drinking and dancing like we do in our weekends. These people however are free of stress. Marriage is the most important moment in their lives. Estrangement doesn't bother them; they would not have a provision for it. Divorce is not an option; they won't understand what it means. I wished I could speak to the man. I wished I could tell him how privileged he was. I saw the familiar signs of the settlement. Everybody around welcomed us. Rimi must have been busy sitting with the women. I did not see any signs of her. The others helped my mate take the macaw off his shoulders. It was immediately carried by two men into a large hut. I could see some smoke coming out of it already. I wondered whether the monkey would be smoked or curried. A few kids ran to me with some stones in their hands. When close enough they jumped on their feet. I tried to understand what kind of greeting that was. Each of them was desperate to hand over the stones to me. I wondered whether it was an excitement upon seeing me or a real game. I did not want to offend any of the kids by showing favour. I took the handful from one of them.

The others stood silently and made a sad and drooping face. I followed the kid to a spot. He sat on his knees. The small piece of ground there did not have any signs of grass. It was clean and dry mud. It had the impressions of some shapes. I thought it must be some game like we had the dice games when we were small.

"Tina tina". The kid said.

I understood by his gesture that he was asking me to sit. I sat across him. The rest of the kids gathered all around us.

"Tonga, tonga, tonga." They kept repeating.

I hardly knew what that meant. 'Come on', or 'fight' or 'buck up', something.

The kid spread pebbles around. He picked them and arranged them in some fashion. The large and small pebbles alternated each other. Fine, I understood something. He picked a small piece up between his nimble fingers and after a long flight in the air touching the stones, he landed it at a blank square. I did not understand what he did.

"Tonga, tonga." The pack shrieked again.

I looked at them, dazzled, confused. I picked a large piece up. The boys did not object, meaning that the larger ones belonged to me. I felt the boys bent further down to see where I was moving it, eyes wide open. I touched it over a few pieces, with a super man sound 'whoo' and like a master crafter landed it in an empty block.

"Anka kita houa, anka keeno." A boy expressed in a rebellious voice. The boy across me picked the pebble I moved and put it back, where it came from. All the hard work for nothing; I wasn't getting any discount. I hid my face in my palms. The boys grabbed my shoulders and shook me.

"Tonga, tonga." They all said.

"I don't know how to move. Teach me." I said with gestures. It didn't help.

"Tonga, tonga."

I looked back. There was no help around. It was these boys against me. I didn't even have a candy on me to bribe one of them to play for me. I held the hands of the sweetest and the youngest kid and made him sit next to me. I gestured that with all my means that I needed help. He gazed at me in an unbelievable expression. I knew what he meant.

"You are the stupidest person on earth. You don't know how to play this game." He said in his language. The rest laughed and supported him.

"Can't a grown up man learn from a kid?" I replied in my language, with the same fervour. "Consider that I am just born here, a newly landed kid."

The kids stopped laughing and tried listening to me very carefully. They followed every gesture of mine. I knew they were trying to.

"Help me learn. Would you do the same thing to your infant brothers?"

"Tonga, tonga." I was disappointed. My efforts were going waste.

The kid on my side then picked another large piece up and moved it to a block. It went on for a few minutes. Suddenly the kid on the other side stood up and shouted in joy. I concluded that the other boy had won. Another boy fought with him and took his spot. He stared straight at me while arranging the pebbles again. The thought of another game scared me more than any thing else at that moment. I looked on both my sides, stood up and ran.

"Achoong kino?" The boys asked in turn.

I never replied and kept running until I found the first man. The boys followed me. They conversed with the man. I thought they conveyed how stupid I was. I thought I should play with them some easier game. I really wanted to play with them. I gestured a boy to hand over his pebbles to me. I took all of them in my hand. I found a rock and placed at a clean spot. Next I gave the boy back all the larger pebbles. I held six and aimed at the bigger rock one after another. I missed the target five out of six times. The boys were watching me. I collected all the pebbles and handed him to the boy I borrowed it from and asked him to do the same. He aimed and hit the target five out of six times. I picked the kid up in my arms and raised his hand. The other kids gathered around me and jumped in glee. I put him down and selected two more kids. I counted six of the smaller pebbles again and hand it over to the first kid. He tried his turn. Four out of six. His opponent tried. Five out of six. I picked the second kid up and gave him the same joyous shake. I ran around with him in my arms, our arms extended as we ran in circles. I had an idea. I should let the winner stay and pick the best winner up. I contested the winner each time with a new kid. A few men gathered around to watch us play. They joined us. I pooled the men in the game too. Slowly I could see some women too. While we were happily laughing and frolicking, I never noticed when it started growing darker. I saw the moon below the horizon. It suddenly reminded me of the night when I and Rimi were watching the forest fires. I looked around for her. I thought I saw the fall of her apron between a few women, but couldn't make her out. I followed that movement, but I lost it. I got back to the game. Everybody already knew what the rules were. They were playing among themselves. I held the arms of an elderly woman and pulled her to the contest ground. Everybody gazed at me, as if I had done the biggest crime. I pulled another lady and let them contest each other. I brought a small girl next and then more women. I pulled the young kids to contest the women. Slowly the men and the women were playing each other. It was uproar. The light was entirely gone. I gestured the man, I knew him by his name then, 'Kumku'. I pat him on his shoulders and asked him if we should make the fire. We made the huge fire. It was the same log of wood that I had pieced up in the morning. It was my hard work. We made the fire. I didn't know how to strike stones, I watched them light the wood dust first and then the log of wood. I was learning. I thought I would attempt the next day. By the time I went back to the game, the women were gone. I wondered where Rimi was. I thought I would teach the kids some of the more conventional games, like hide and seek. In a few moments they were all hiding and I was the one looking for them. I was busted every time, even before I arrested the first few kids hiding. I saw Kumku carrying some stuff in a pot. I stopped him and said that I wanted to talk to him. I was picking up their language.

"Do you know where Rimi is?" I tried to say in language half broken and half gestures.

"Tinni?" He asked.

I remembered Tinni means woman. I nodded head.

He said something that I did not entirely understand, but he made a glum face. I assumed something was wrong. Anxiety was killing me. I really wanted to see her. I wanted to make sure she was fine. I asked him if I could go and see her. It took me a minute to explain. He nodded his head in a straight no. I pleaded. He then asked me to be silent and follow him. He took me around one of the huts, a little distance from there. I heard Rimi's voice with some other women. He peeked inside through the gaps. It was dark behind us. The door was on the other side, towards the large bonfire. I peeked in too. I saw her. She was happily laughing away, enjoying. They were treating her like a princess and there I was. I felt jealous again. I started saying something to Kumku but he shut me up right away. We ran back the way we came from, back to the pot he was carrying.

"Can you wait for a second?" I put my hands on his shoulders gesturing while I talked.

"What is it?" He replied back.

"Can you take me to Glian? I want to see him." I meekly said.

"He won't see you." He shook his head.

"But why?" I asked back.

"Choome tikko tinni" He just stared hard at me.

I understood what he meant. I did not respect my woman.

"But she isn't my woman. We are just neighbours, friends." I tried to explain.

He kept staring at me. As if I had done a very shameful thing and was being further mean by not accepting it.

"Huh." I thought. "How do things work around here? Is everybody insane here?" I spoke in plain English.

My expressions might have looked nasty. He walked away with the pot. There were more men around but I felt so lonely. I wanted to run away yet again. I always ran away from the cities to the forests and mountains, but at that moment I wanted to escape somewhere farther where I would not have to match any expectations. Somewhere where I won't need to explain my acts, I and only I would be responsible for my actions; away from any kind of human colonies. I had been there with the tribe for two days and was already living like them. I was adaptable. I could learn anything in this world. If one man could do something, I could too. I stood there watching the clear sky, the stars. I wondered what it must be like when it rained. It would be such a tough situation. Did the bamboo huts leak? The soil must get soggy, how did they deal with that? What about insects? So much of infection could spread around in those moments, and these people, did not even have a physician. They had the pritimive medicines, mortared out of herbs, wood, insects, but how could that be enough? Humans are so prone to fall sick. Then I corrected myself. These people were not regular humans. They were not infested with sickness. They weren't city dwellers. They did not munch on McDs and use soft drinks to force it down their throats. They did not watch violence on television and clap their hands. They did not take anti depressants and survive on aspirin. They were healthy humans. They could certainly fall sick but the probability would be as low as that of a tiger or any other wild animal. How many times could a tiger fall sick in its life? How many times does a man from the cities fall sick in his life? I thought about evolution. An animal can adapt to his surroundings capably and man is at its prime at that front. In the name of evolution man has only grown weaker and weaker. He is mentally weak; physically, he is a warehouse of diseases. Where are we heading? What is next? I felt happy. I wasn't breathing carbon infested air, I wasn't polluting my senses with synthetic music. The food I ate wasn't coming from the cultured farms. I was so close to nature. Like Glian. I looked around for Kumku again. We could understand each other best. I asked each of the men around. At last, I found him skinning a boar.

"Kumku, Kumku." I expressed in excitement.

He looked at me.

"I am ready to marry her." I forgot to add gestures to my words.

He looked back at me strangely thinking that I was trying to be funny again. Then I explained to him what I meant. His eyes expanded. He wasn't really ready to believe that I just said that.

"Can I see Glian now?"

"Yeah, yeah. Later tonight. He would be very glad." Kumku called one of the men and sent him off somewhere.

I sat next to Kumku, helping him skin the animal. I had done all that earlier, not with a boar though.

He said something to the rest of the men and all of them looked at me with their faces full of smiles. I felt happy at that moment. A union is such a happy moment for them. But truly, I did feel close to Rimi.

Skinning the boar was hard work. Upon seeing that I was doing a good job, Kumku handed me another freshly killed boar. That I thought would be tough. A boar had a thick skin and that too a wild one. The pair of tusks jutting out from its jaw, made its looks scary. I worked on it. I did a pretty bad job that time. Kumku finished it.

"Pretty bad work. You need to learn." He said.

"I do."

Kumku picked the first boar up and tied its legs to a bamboo, in pairs. It tied the other one next to it. He asked me to pick one end up, while he picked the other end up. We carried the bambooed boars on our shoulders. The fire was just ready. It had a pair of bamboos sitting in a cross at two ends. We softly placed bamboo with the boars on the crossed saddles. It was fun. Everybody had a role to play, like a colony of ants.

A meeting was called in the night. Glian sat on a cane chair. The fire was at the centre. Everybody including me, sat around. The women were behind him. I still couldn't see Rimi.

Glian announced that the boy and the girl from the city would be married the next day. Everybody stood up and waved their arms in the air in appreciation.

"They will be married at noon." Glian contined.

Everybody stood up again and hailed him.

"The boy has to give four boars in dowry." Glian looked straight at me. His brows were knitted. His forehead shone the distinct lines of experience. Everybody was silent as soon as he said it. I didn't understand what he said. Kumku explained it to me.

"Boars." I thought. "Does everybody have to give boars as dowry." I asked Kemku.

"Yes, he answered."

"But how will I find them and that too before tomorrow noon?" I asked him back.

"In the forest; I showed you how we hunt. Every body however has to give two boars. I think Glian is testing you."

"Testing me? Heaven and hell. I have to find boars to clear a test. Ridiculous."

"He wants to see if you are serious about the marriage."

I looked at Glian. We stared hard at each other. He had given me an impossible task. I looked back at him with acceptance. I would put all in me to find the boars.

"You must leave now." Kumku said. "You don't have a lot of time."

"I am hungry. I need to eat something." I replied.

"Wait for me at the stream." I will be there in some time.

"Would I have to go hunting alone? How can I do it?"

"I will get some food for you. I will give you the bamboo and darts, but I can't help you beyond that."

"I am not even a good shooter with that bamboo. I am skeptical."

"Don't argue." Kumku added.

I saw Glian shake his head.

"Glian wants you to leave now."

15

The hunt for boars

I walked to the stream. I saw different facets of moon on the face of the stream. I had noticed the big peaceful image before, but never had I sat with it in peace. How did it feel when there was no body around but only heavenly bodies? Did one want to talk to them? I wish I could. I could talk to them. The darkness and light seemed to play with each other. I was a part of this, chiruscuro. I was borrowing something from everything around me, each moment. I looked at the moon again for assurance. It was there for me, always. It wouldn't go away in my life time. I could think of the moon as something real as well as, immortal. A living creature around me more substantial than another human being. My life time was an eternity for me. What was it that has lived before me and will live after me? All the smaller things were so trite. It had been watching over us for zillions of years. It had seen world wars, battles for wealth, kingdoms, women; it knew it all. People had come and gone. I was there for the moment, next moment I would be gone. I would fight a war, struggle in a job, bring back home a grumble, shout at my parents, my close ones. I lived in a closed box. That box had a hole, a very small hole. There was light everywhere outside. The hole was yellow during the day and white in the nights. It lit up the inside, but I had taken it for granted. I did not question myself. The crickets around me sounded an infinite agreement. Perhaps they understood what I was thinking. The fire flies shimmered in gusts. They reflected the light from the moon. I felt something crawling on my neck. I was too absorbed to react. I let it be there. It slowly descended on my arms and down my body; it crawled away. I realized it was a small snake. It did not disturb me. It thought I was a part of nature. I felt happy upon being given so much of respect. I wasn't being labelled an alien. It was a perfect camouflage for me. I was learning to disappear. I was learning to give up my man made identity. I felt I was no longer Dev. It was much like the ink stamp on paper that washes away in water. What remains is the white paper again. I was that white paper. I crouched farther into the tree. I felt the roots. I knew millions of insects would be crawling around, but none of them would bother me. I respected their existence. They were not just insects; they were nature, a part of the big existence, a part of the earth, a part of the sun, moon, the solar system, the entire galaxy. I was a part of it too. For a moment I disliked being called Dev. I liked the name Glian. Who named the leader Glian? What must have his parents thought? His parents were so much more aware than my parents. They knew so much more. They prevailed in not knowing. Not knowing is more knowledgeable than knowing what is false and crafted. A blank, a zero, where we all belonged. I felt some liquid drop on my face. I brushed it with my finger and smelled it. It smelled sweet. I tasted it. Bats must have been carrying fruits around. More of the liquid dropped over me. I noticed bats screech. I looked up and saw a swarm of them flying, taking refuge in the tree I was sitting under. Perhaps they were picking the fruits from it. It was such a pleasant feeling. I wanted to be one of them, fly with them into the open skies. Feel the gust in the highest of the skies. I wanted to go so high up where the sun and moon would never set. For a moment I blamed the rotation of the earth for creating the illusion of motion. I counted days and nights with each appearance of the sun. But it never actually set. It's always there, immovable, the same, infinite during my life time. What was moving then? Nothing. I was a part of a big static system. I was living in illusion. I thought I was going to work, but was I? I thought I felt learned when I could read and write, but was I actually learned? I thought I was doing the world a service, but was I? Was I not doing anything, actually?

"Jojo Tinna." Kumku's voice floated, dragging me out of the world I was comfortable in.

Jojo meant come.

"Here." I stood up immediately.

He had a few things in hands. I could smell the roasted meat. He gave it to me, the first thing. He watched me eat it. A perfect dinner; no lamps, no lights. He gave me a thick stick, a belt with some darts tied to it and the small bamboo gun.

"We have to find the boars. It takes a long time to find them." He said.

"Would I have to do it alone?"

"Yes."

I went to the stream and drank some water, picking up a handful each time. I came back to Kumku.

"You will do it." He patted my shoulders.

"Where do I start?" I was nervous.

"I will come along with you."

"But you just said that I have to do it alone."

"You have to hunt alone. I will show you the way."

I was standing next to another teacher. They come when they are most needed. I stuck to him in an overwhelming embrace and cried. I felt I had known him since eternity. He returned my embrace. I had found my first friend there.

He led me to the jungle. We watched out for the smallest of motions.

"Boars are usually huddled together at nights. They walk around when the night starts and then sleep to end it."

"Is there any place where we can find them?"

"We have to look."

We looked for them. We had travelled for three hours before we found the first one. I took position quickly with the bamboo and a dart, but I missed it. We had lost them.

"You have to blow the dart real hard on boars. They have a very thick skin."

"But I am pretty bad at aiming."

"Don't worry. I am with you." He assured me in the voice of the teacher.

For the rest of the night we kept hunting. The sun was up and we had only one boar. We were wandering in the jungle and I was tired. I looked at Kumku, he did not have the slightest trace of weariness on his face. He looked as fresh as ever. By the time it was late in the morning we had just three of them. I was still short by one.

"We have to go back." Kumku said. "They must be waiting at the ceremony."

"But we still have to find the last one."

"I have kept one for you." He laughed as he said. "Make sure that you tell no one that I went out with you."

I promised my teacher that everything stayed between us. When we reached back to the settlement, Kumku added the last one to my heap. All four of them were tied to my stick. I held the loaded pole horizontally across the back of my neck, like that macaw. It was heavy. The men surrounded me, beating the ground with their legs. They led me to the ceremonial grounds. I reached there and threw the boars on the ground. I couldn't carry them any longer. I lay on the ground. I couldn't stand any more. The men helped me stand and walk. I saw Glian standing in front of me, through my half shut eyes. I have a very poor memory of what happened at the ceremony. I remember being seated on a bamboo seat, but I think I passed out. I remember waking up next morning. A few women were next to me, perhaps nursing me. They were shoving some powdery herb in my mouth. It tasted bitter, that's what might have woken me up. It was the bitterest thing I ever had; considering that I was always very fond of bitter gourd. I saw Rimi sitting near my head. I felt relieved. She was in the same khaki apron.

"Are we married?" I asked her when I got a moment alone with her.

"What do you think?"

"I feel like the same old man. I don't even know what happened."

"Did you accept me within yourself?"

"Within myself?" I thought. "Yes; long back, the hunt for the boars made me even more resolute." I took a moment to think and answer.

"Then I am your wife. It doesn't matter what happened at the ceremony."

"But was it good? I missed it entirely."

"Very good."

"And everybody let me be unconscious while we married. Did nobody notice that I needed attention?"

"Do you want to fight?"

"Yes."

"Let me make it easy for you then. The ceremony never happened. They did the bare essentials."

One of the women then came in, carrying with her some more of the herbs. I stopped asking Rimi questions.

Among all the women, I felt I could distuinguish her smell. I was feeling sick. It took me two days to recover. I had some kind of a bad fever. I had no hard feelings about it, as long as Rimi was next to me. Glian came to see me once. He said he was proud of me. The men later told me that I was one of the rare few who Glian ever praised. I was held in very high esteem after that. I was considered a close cohort to him. Two days later I had enough strength to walk. The men helped me walk to my hut. When we were close to the hut, Rimi took over and helped me get in. I lay down again as soon as I went in.

"So you are my wife." I said.

Rimi smiled. I slept off again. I woke up again in the evening, feeling strong. Kumku was sitting next to me. He helped me have some water. Rimi got some food for me. She fed me with her hands. I bit her fingers and apologized vigorously. She asked me to eat myself when I bit her the second time. I refused to eat unless she fed me. The night came. Glian same to see me again.

"Glian, I am feeling strong enough now."

Rimi and Kumku were sitting with us.

"Good for you."

"Can I leave for home tomorrow?"

"Do you really want to leave so early?"

"It's been a long time. People must be worried."

"Alright as you say. I will get your things ready for you by tomorrow morning."

"Really? Can I get my watch and camera back?"

"Yes, you will."

He left. I kept thinking about what I would do when I got back. I was so privileged to have gone through the entire experience.

"Rimi, don't you feel wonderful? We had such a happy stay here."

She nodded.

"And we are married too."

She nodded again.

"No I really mean it. I have really accepted you as my wife. We can go back and register ourselves."

"I don't care for that filthy piece of paper. Remember what you said about marriages?"

"Yes, I do. Neither do I believe in those pieces of paper."

"Do you really want us to leave so soon?"

"What? Are you really asking that question?"

She did not answer.

"It's just a momentary love for the surroundings, Rimi. It will be the most convenient thing to stay back, at this point of time, for some more time. But think about the things we need to do, responsibilities we need to meet."

She again nodded.

I had entirely forgotten in that period of time that I had gotten so much used to staying naked like the tribes men. I felt comfortable. I did not feel the need for clothes. It had become so natural for me. We talked about the forest and what Rimi had done in the last three days as the night went deeper into darkness.

"Don't you feel uncomfortable in that thing?"

"What thing?"

"In that apron of yours?"

She was sitting next to me. She shook her head in disagreement.

She stood up and took a couple of steps. She opened the strings to the apron on her shoulders and let the apron fall to the ground. She was standing entirely naked in front of me. I watched her. She spread her arms and stood there in joy.

"I was waiting for this day when I could let this final thing slip off and be like you." She mumbled.

I knew what she meant. We were both extensions of nature then. A part of nature; as we were supposed to be. There were no lies, no deceit, no presumptions, no prejudices, no hypocrisy. We made love the entire night. The call of the owls, crickets, the humble breeze, frogs croaking, all approved of our union.

I woke up next day in the morning, all set to pack and leave. I met Glian, Kumku, the men, the women, the children and bowed to everybody, everything there to take my leave. I thanked everybody for the generosity. I picked our bags up. I wore my spare clothes and was glad to wear my watch again. Rimi was nowhere to be seen however. I went back to my hut and found Rimi weeping.

"What happened? C'mon we have to leave. It's a long way." I addressed her.

She took to a long silence. Her heavy and crushing sobs were enough to choke her throat. I understood she was feeling bad.

"I don't want to leave now. Let's live for a few more days."

"A few more days? What difference would it make? Today, tomorrow, it has to be some day." I cradled her head in my chest while I made sure that I was being very soft with her.

I lost. Her womaliness had won over me. I decided to stay a few more days. The days turned into months. We hadn't left. The arguments over leaving for home had faded.

"What home?" I occasionally asked myself.

A year later a beautiful baby was born to us; a son. We named him Glian, after the leader and more than that, he was the true son of nature.

Little Glian was four years old when one day a white man appeared with a *titake.*

I shook hands with him and told him our story. He was glad to meet Rimi.

"Do you ever plan to go back?"

I did not have an answer. Perhaps a 'no' would have been more appropriate. He asked me to write my experiences down so it could be shared with the world. I was encouraged. He gave me two blank note books and I scribbled on it, for ten long days. I exhausted five ball pens. And here I am at the point where I am writing, in the present. It was hard writing everything down. Two reason, I was used to let the keys on my computer do the writing, and I hadn't written anything in the last five years. How did I know it was five years? I had seen five summers, five winters and five rainy seasons. But I can be mistaken, it can also be six or four. I can't take the word for how old little Glian is. His mother says that he is four years old. We don't know his birthdate. My watch did carry dates, but it had run out of batteries, before he was born. I had used too much of the GPS. I however saw happy

Glian play with the kids in the tribe. He was one of them. He played with animals, birds, wind, stream, flowers.

By the time you gentlemen and women read this, Glian would have grown older. You know much more than he does. You have more knowledge than he does. But like I say, sometimes, not knowing is more knowledgeable than knowing. I am depriving him of everything that is unnatural. He doesn't watch television like you do, doesn't play computer games, doesn't wear Armani Xchange (I still remember the brand), isn't growing to watch sex videos, but certainly he can talk to birds, animals, trees, flowers. He wouldn't have to try hard for board exams, look for a job, live a stressful life, hating people. He will catch butterflies all his life, like I still do. In depriving him from the city, no, your city, I am given him a true life. Life, as it should have been. I will watch Glian grow in the arms of nature and relive my childhood, in all the things I missed. Glian, is the true son of nature. And what happened to Arthur? Let's ask Rini. She is dusting the floor mat right on my face.

"Rini, what happened to our Arthur? Did we find him?" I ask her.

"What Aurthr? Haven't you found him already?" She replies.

I laugh back at her. Isn't there a Arthur in each of us?

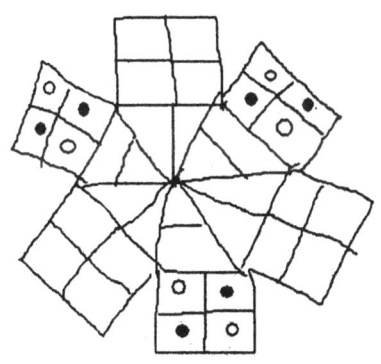

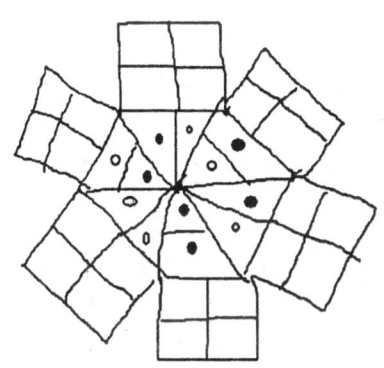